♡ Jamie Kiffe

EXPLORER ACADEMY

FUTURE TECH

THE SCIENCE BEHIND THE STORY

JAMIE KIFFEL-ALCHEH

NATIONAL GEOGRAPHIC
WASHINGTON, D.C.

FUTURE TECH

TABLE OF CONTENTS

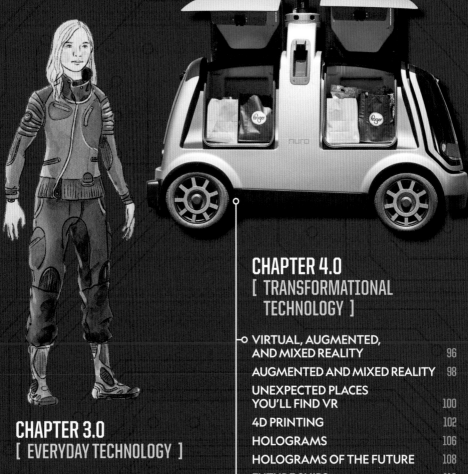

CHAPTER 4.0
[TRANSFORMATIONAL TECHNOLOGY]

CHAPTER 3.0
[EVERYDAY TECHNOLOGY]

WHAT IS THIS
BOOK ABOUT?

Mood-reading glasses ... thought-controlled clothing ... robotic bees ... do those things exist? They do in the near-future world of Explorer Academy, an elite school where 12-year-old Cruz Coronado and his fellow recruits train to become the world's next great researchers and adventurers. At the Academy, he and his teammates take on exciting missions, like excavating a lost city, rescuing a pod of endangered right whales, and camera-trapping animal poachers. Cruz also has his own top secret mission—to find and collect eight stone puzzle pieces that his mother hid around the world while she was alive. Together, these cipher pieces reveal the formula she invented for a cell-regenerating serum that could help millions of people. But one greedy, mysterious organization, Nebula, will do anything to destroy that formula—even if it means destroying Cruz himself.

Luckily for Cruz, he and his friends take on their adventures with the most cutting-edge technology the world has to offer. And even cooler? It's created at Explorer Academy, by some of the planet's top scientists—and students!

You will soon have the chance to unleash your inner explorer because in this book you're a part of the action. You'll envision yourself as a new recruit trying on a mind-reading headset, seeing a 3D hologram, getting inside the Computer Animated Virtual Environment (CAVE), and experiencing all the other tech an explorer like Cruz would get to use. Wish it was real? Keep reading. Almost all the technology featured in this series is inspired by sci-entific discoveries from actual scientists and inventors, many of whom are National Geographic explorers. Thanks to this terrific tech, the future is now. So, get ready to feast your eyes on everything from real-life RoboBees, like Mell, to lifesaving venoms, submersible discoveries, and much more. After all, the near-future world of Explorer Academy is just across the horizon, and much of its tech is already shaping our world.

Welcome to the jaw-dropping world of future tech!

WEARABLE TECH

At Explorer Academy, you slip on a jacket so thin, it feels like you're wearing a second skin. Moments later, it's shrinking, contracting, until you barely notice it ... because it's resizing itself to conform to your exact shape! This specialized outfit can fend off bugs, reptiles, and much more. But if you do get into a scrape during one of your missions, there's also a band around your wrist that tracks your vital signs and pings a doctor the moment it registers you're hurt.

Wearable technology is everywhere, and it's more advanced every day. Check out some of the most exciting wearable tech in Explorer Academy, and see how it stacks up against real inventions, like smart wristbands, shape-changing glasses, techie temporary tattoos, and more.

SPECIAL DIVING HELMETS ALLOW PEOPLE TO BREATHE UNDERWATER.

HEART-MONITORING WRISTBAND
[ORGANIC SYNCHRONIZATION BAND]

HOW IT WORKS AT THE ACADEMY

When you arrive at the Academy, adviser Taryn Secliff asks you to hold out your left wrist. There's a flash of gold, and something wraps around your arm. It's a skinny band that automatically adjusts to the size of your wrist. Taryn says it's called an "OS" or "Organic Synchronization" band, but most students call it the "Open Sesame." That's because it's a digital key to most security points on the Explorer Academy campus and aboard the Academy's ship, *Orion*. It can identify you based on your heartbeat! Bonus: It'll monitor your vital signs, physical activity, calorie intake, brain function, growth patterns, and general health. It also tells the time.

You're sure to put the OS band to good use during your time at the Academy, just like Cruz does. In Book 3: *The Double Helix*, Cruz is trapped at the bottom of a cave filled with skulls near Aksaray, Turkey. Bruised, starving, and stuck in complete darkness without his computer tablet or communication pin, Cruz feels pretty hopeless. But then, a crackling voice calls his name from ... his wrist?! It's his trusty OS band, which has a surprising, very handy additional function—communication.

HOW IT WORKS IN REAL LIFE

Although no band can do everything OS bands can do—*yet*—Open Sesames aren't the only wristbands with communication, fitness tracking, and medical capabilities.

Seizure-stopper

Embrace is a wristband that detects body changes that might signal a seizure, and immediately pings family, friends, or caregivers. It even sends your GPS location so helpers can find you quickly. Sensors in the device do this by picking up changes in your pulse, motion, temperature, and electrical signals. It's even waterproof so you can wear it in the bath!

Unique opener

The Nymi Band can use your electro-cardiogram—that's a heart-rate reading, also called an EKG—as your password. Press your finger to an electrode on top of the device, and the band will measure tiny bursts of electricity sent from your heart through your pulse. Those bursts create a heartbeat pattern that's unique to you. Nymi can send that information wirelessly to locked devices that have been paired with it, and ... open sesame!

MORE EKGs AT YOUR FINGERTIPS

At a hospital, taking an EKG usually requires the use of wires called "leads," sensors, and messy gel. But KardiaMobile 6L, which looks like a silvery stick of gum, delivers a six-lead EKG through a medical-grade device! Just rest it on your leg and hold both sides for a reading—three electrodes will pick up your data. If the device detects an abnormal rhythm, it's time to call the doctor.

THERMOCHROMIC MATERIALS
[EMOTO-GLASSES]

HOW IT WORKS AT THE ACADEMY

You're in the Explorer Academy dining hall, about to eat a forkful of waffles with whipped cream and strawberries, when you overhear someone saying there's a quiz today in your archaeology class. You forgot to review! As your pulse races, something happens. The glasses you're wearing bend and twist, changing from green circles to black-and-white streaked trapezoids. That's because they're emoto-glasses, and they transform when they detect changes in your mood!

In Book 1: *The Nebula Secret*, Cruz's roommate Emmett Lu explains how he invented emoto-glasses by injecting neurotransmitter nanoprocessors into his bloodstream. They tell his glasses how much dopamine, serotonin, and noradrenaline (aka neurotransmitters) are in his body. Since neurotransmitter levels change with mood, the glasses receive cues to change color and shape depending on how Emmett feels.

As for how he crafted the specialized specs, Emmett printed them on a 4D printer, where the fourth "D" stands for time—that is, the time it takes the material to change after it's been printed! 4D materials are programmed to transform when they come in contact with triggers like water, heat, or, in Emmett's case, a cue from a nanoprocessor. (Find out more about 4D printing on page 102.)

MAYBE FEASIBLE

FEASIBLE

FEASIBILITY SCALE

[EMOTO-GLASSES] FEASIBILITY SCALE

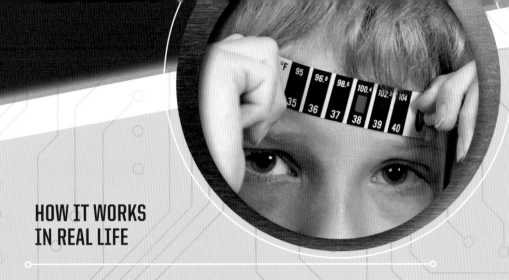

HOW IT WORKS IN REAL LIFE

Neural microsensors similar to the ones Emmett uses already exist. Implantable microsensors are used to monitor neurotransmitter levels in patients with neurological disorders. There are no glasses that change colors and shapes by connecting to your brain's impulses the way emoto-glasses do. But there are real materials that spontaneously change colors, and they don't need to sync with brain signals to do it. They're called thermochromic materials, and they can turn into a rainbow of shades in seconds!

Crystals and Color Changes

Developed in the 1960s and named after the Greek words for "heat" and "color," thermochromic materials work in a few different ways. Some contain billions of microscopic capsules. Inside the capsules are liquid crystals that rearrange, making them look like different colors at different temperatures.

Leuco Dyes

Other thermochromic materials are called leuco dyes. They're named after the Greek word *leukos*, which means "white." When carbon molecules inside them react to changes in light, heat, or pH (acidity level), the molecules change structure, going from white to full color.

BEFORE

Glasses for Every Occasion

National Geographic Explorer Skylar Tibbits has worked on glasses a lot like Emmett's, and his version can also change shapes. "So you have one pair of glasses that can work for a party or for going to a business meeting," says Tibbits. (Read more about Tibbits' shape-changing work on page 103.)

AFTER

THESE BEADS USE LEUCO DYE TECHNOLOGY TO CHANGE COLOR WHEN EXPOSED TO SUNLIGHT.

TEMPERATURE-CHANGING
TIMELINE

[Thermochromic Materials Throughout History]

1970s

MOOD RINGS
These rings start out black, but change colors as you wear them. Makers claim that the different colors reveal different moods, but actually, the colors are from liquid crystals reacting to your body heat!

1980s

LEGAL DOCUMENTS THAT CHANGE COLOR WITH TOUCH TO PROVE THEY'RE AUTHENTIC
Is that million-dollar check for real? Warming heat-sensitive chromatic paper between your fingers can reveal a seal of authenticity that's hard to reproduce.

1990s

HYPERCOLOR T-SHIRTS
These shirts start out one color, then turn a second color when they warm up with your body heat, thanks to leuco dyes. Major minus: They got brightest around warm armpits.

2000s

UV-REACTIVE COLOR CHANGE NAIL POLISH
Temperature-sensitive dye turns the paint one color, and UV from sunshine reacts with photochromic powder in the paint to turn it a second color.

2010s

COLOR-CHANGING CAR PAINT

Temperature makes this car paint change color. With a car coated in this paint, Nebula could drive away in a red car, then make a quick disguise by turning the car black. A splash of cold water is all it takes!

FACTORY PIPES WITH COLOR-CHANGING INDICATORS

These pipes turn colors to warn workers when the water running through them is dangerously hot.

TODAY

SKIN-SAVING TEMPORARY TATTOOS

National Geographic Explorer Skylar Tibbits co-founded LogicInk, a company that makes UV-sensitive temporary tattoos. Too much UV can lead to skin cancer, so the outer circle and bar of the tattoo turn pink to signal when it's time to get out of the sun!

THE FUTURE

COLOR-CHANGING HOUSE PAINT

A house that turns white in the heat will stay cooler and save energy!

MILITARY CAMOUFLAGE

A special kind of liquid crystal is being studied for its ability to change clothing's colors within very narrow temperature ranges. A soldier might be able to turn jungle-green in the rainforest like Bryndis does, and ice-white in an ice cave, like Emmett!

CLOAKING TECHNOLOGY & MIND CONTROL
[LUMAGINE SHADOW BADGE]

HOW IT WORKS AT THE ACADEMY

You look down at your sweatshirt and jeans. They're comfortable, but kind of blah. What if you could instantly change their color? You glance at the shimmery Lumagine sticker on your collar and tap it twice, then picture your favorite shade and fabric as clearly as you can. Your clothes start to roll and flicker. Then, they morph into the precise color and texture you were imagining!

Lumagine is a mind-activated tool that Emmett Lu invents (yup, it's named after him) with help from tech lab chief Dr. Fanchon Quills. It can change the color, pattern, and texture of anything you wear. All you have to do is think about it. Tapping the Lumagine badge twice releases a bio-net that surrounds the wearer, then syncs up with nerve fibers in the wearer's brain. In Book 4: *The Star Dunes*, Lumagine's forest camouflage helps Bryndis and other recruits deliver medication to sick mountain gorillas without scaring them away.

But Lumagine really shines, so to speak, when it can't be seen. In Book 2: *The Falcon's Feather*, Emmett is trapped in an Icelandic cave with Cruz, Bryndis, and Sailor. He's desperate for a way out that won't alert armed Nebula agents. One tap of his Lumagine badge camouflages and makes him invisible, just like a real-life superhero!

[LUMAGINE]
FEASIBILITY SCALE

MAYBE FEASIBLE
FEASIBLE
FEASIBILITY SCALE

HOW IT WORKS IN REAL LIFE

You already know that fabrics can change color (read all about it on page 13!). But what about making you disappear?

Invisibility Tech

"Spectral cloaking" is a new way to make objects seem invisible. ("Spectral" means "ghostly.") Normally, we see objects when light bounces off them. Spectral cloaking devices change light's frequency so it passes *through* an object instead of bouncing off it, making it look like nothing is there!

Right now, only one-dimensional objects have been made invisible using this technology. But its creators hope that one day it will hide cars, military planes, and even people.

Mind Control

One of the coolest things about Lumagine might be the way it connects with the brain. And mind-reading technology does exist. Test subjects at the University of Toronto Scarborough were hooked up to an electro-encephalogram machine (EEG), the kind of machine that hospitals use to study electrical patterns in the brain. Then, the subjects looked at pictures of people's faces.

THE UNIVERSITY OF TORONTO SCARBOROUGH STUDY USING AN EEG MACHINE

The EEG recorded their brain activity. Using that information, another computer was able to reproduce the pictures the volunteers were seeing in their minds!

WANT MORE?

Cortical recording implants are tiny electrodes that can send or receive brain signals. They've enabled paralyzed people to move prosthetic limbs just by thinking about it! (Read about more mind-reading tech on page 30.)

SMART ACCESSORIES & INTELLIGENT TEXTILES

[EXPLORER ACADEMY STUDENT UNIFORM]

HOW IT WORKS AT THE ACADEMY

So far, you've been wearing everyday clothes for your missions. But today, you got a huge surprise. You get to try on your Explorer Academy uniform! Dr. Fanchon Quills explains that the jacket doubles as a flotation device and has a parachute hidden in the back. There's also an EA pin on the jacket collar. You press it, then jump when it answers, "Yes? This is Taryn." Adviser Taryn Secliff explains that the pin is a communicator that can call anyone else with an EA pin, and it also works as a global translator if you press the pin twice. Now you can speak every language *and* look pretty cool while you're at it.

Here's the tech each Explorer Academy uniform has inside it, and real-life inventions **that are just as cool!**

Sun ray blocker
EXISTS! Products like Solumbra fabric boast 100+ SPF, which blocks more than 99 percent of damaging sun rays.

Flotation device
EXISTS! Flotation jackets, also called "float coats," are Coast Guard–approved flotation devices with buoyant foam inside.

Water-repellent fabric
EXISTS! Ottertex (named after water-repellent otters!) is canvas made of polyester. It's backed in polyvinyl chloride (PVC), which makes it totally waterproof.

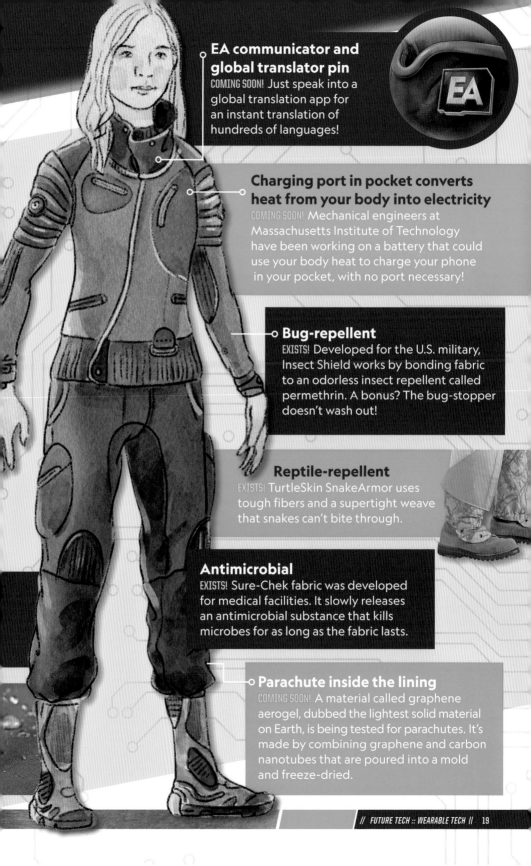

EA communicator and global translator pin
COMING SOON! Just speak into a global translation app for an instant translation of hundreds of languages!

Charging port in pocket converts heat from your body into electricity
COMING SOON! Mechanical engineers at Massachusetts Institute of Technology have been working on a battery that could use your body heat to charge your phone in your pocket, with no port necessary!

Bug-repellent
EXISTS! Developed for the U.S. military, Insect Shield works by bonding fabric to an odorless insect repellent called permethrin. A bonus? The bug-stopper doesn't wash out!

Reptile-repellent
EXISTS! TurtleSkin SnakeArmor uses tough fibers and a supertight weave that snakes can't bite through.

Antimicrobial
EXISTS! Sure-Chek fabric was developed for medical facilities. It slowly releases an antimicrobial substance that kills microbes for as long as the fabric lasts.

Parachute inside the lining
COMING SOON! A material called graphene aerogel, dubbed the lightest solid material on Earth, is being tested for parachutes. It's made by combining graphene and carbon nanotubes that are poured into a mold and freeze-dried.

BIOLUMINESCENCE
[HIDE-AND-SEEK JACKET]

HOW IT WORKS AT THE ACADEMY

Your Explorer Academy uniform came with a coordinating gray camouflage coat nicknamed the "Hide-and-Seek" jacket. It's after lights out, but you can't resist trying it on. The reversible silver lining seems plain at first. Then you press a button on the collar, and you find out why the jacket got its nickname. The whole coat glows in the dark, making it easy for you to be found!

You're probably going to need this jacket on your own adventures, just like Team Cousteau in Book 2: *The Falcon's Feather*. Trapped deep inside an Icelandic glacier, Cruz, Sailor, and Bryndis can't find a way to send out a communication signal. Nothing can be received or sent from where they are, below the ice. Or can it? Cruz looks up at the ceiling and has an idea. An explosion set off by Nebula blew away a good part of the ice roof. It's got to be thin enough now for light to pass through it! The group piles all its light-up devices in a heap, but that doesn't produce enough shine until the explorers remember their Hide-and-Seek jackets. Not only do the jackets keep the team comfortable in the coldest weather, but they glow like beacons to signal for help, too!

Bioluminescence in Real Life

The Hide-and-Seek jacket uses bioluminescence, which is an actual chemical reaction that produces light in living things. The reaction typically works with two chemicals: luciferin and luciferase. Together, they make light. So how can bioluminescence influence inventions? Here are some bright ideas scientists are exploring.

CITY LIGHTS

Imagine replacing streetlights with trees that light up naturally. Scientists are working on it by developing plants that contain luciferin. Massachusetts Institute of Technology scientists have had some success with watercress so far. The altered plant can shine for nearly four hours!

BRIGHTER WATER

Detecting microscopic water contaminants is complicated. Bioluminescent bacteria can help. They glow less brightly around components from a range of toxins. So the bacteria can be used to test water for the presence of these toxins!

SHINY SUGAR

How about a birthday party where the cake's frosting lights up in your mouth? A company called BioLume is using bioluminescent enzymes to make sweets glow when you eat them. Oxygen and your saliva start the reaction. It's not on the market just yet, but it's sure to be an enlightening treat!

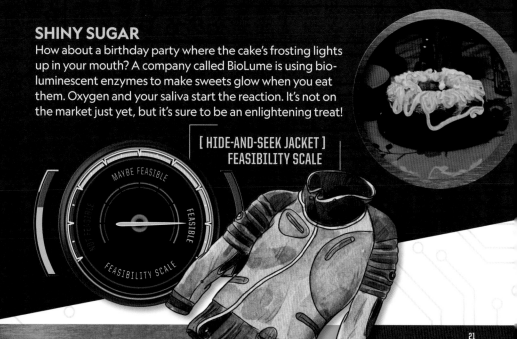

[HIDE-AND-SEEK JACKET]
FEASIBILITY SCALE

MAYBE FEASIBLE
NOT FEASIBLE
FEASIBLE
FEASIBILITY SCALE

ANIMAL LIGHT SHOW

You've probably seen bioluminescence in fireflies, which flash to attract mates. But lots of other creatures are bioluminescent, too! Read on to discover other species that keep the lights on!

FASCINATING FUNGI

Certain fungi produce a spooky, deep-woods glow called foxfire. In some places, it can be bright enough to read by.

LIGHTBULB LURE

The anglerfish uses borrowed bioluminescence to attract and capture prey. Bioluminescent bacteria that grow on the lure hanging from the fish's head draw in curious fish ... then, chomp!

SHINING CEPHALOPOD

Certain types of cephalopods—mollusks like squid, octopuses, and nautiluses—can flash to confuse predators, or spray glowing mucus to send pursuers into a tailspin.

RAINBOW JELLIES

About half of all jellyfish can glow. Some can release their twinkling tentacles to distract predators while the jellyfish swims away.

WILD WORMS

Glowworms are insect larvae that live in caves. They light up to attract other bugs that the larvae can eat.

BRIGHT BACTERIA

Bryndis tells Cruz about the "milky seas," places where bioluminescent bacteria light up the water so brightly that satellites can photograph the effect from their orbit. Off the coast of Somalia, Africa, there's a shining patch as big as the state of Connecticut, U.S.A.

IN SAMUT SAKHON PROVINCE IN THAILAND, BIOLUMINESCENT PLANKTON MAKE THE WATER GLOW.

EXPLORER PROFILE: DAVID F. GRUBER

It's 2 a.m., and dark ocean water laps softly beneath the boat. The sea splashes to life as a diver plunges in. He swishes down to a coral reef where he finds a hidden underwater party. Colored lights are everywhere! The diver is David Gruber, and he's come to study creatures that illuminate the ocean after dark.

Just like Cruz Coronado, Gruber started out as a surfer looking for the best waves. In college, oceanography caught his eye because it seemed like a good way to stay close to the water. But then he started to notice the life beneath his board. It was the light-up creatures he discovered while night diving that hooked him on the underwater world.

Gruber has since become an underwater photographer, submersible designer, professor, and inventor. When he's swimming near sharks, Gruber uses a "shark's-eye" camera he co-developed. It helps him to see fluorescence, a glow that's visible only through certain color and light filters. "Some fish actually have yellow filters in their eyes that accentuate fluorescent objects," says Gruber. This includes some types of catsharks, which glow bright green. "Male and female sharks have different fluorescent patterns, so they're likely using it to signal each other," says Gruber.

Gruber has also worked with scientists to pinpoint fluorescent compounds that can be used as genetic markers, "lighting up" genes of interest (kind of like a highlighter), so that doctors can study how cancer drugs work on them.

ANIMAL ACTION:
THIS TURTLE GLOWS IN THE DARK!

Through his work, David Gruber has helped to find over 200 new species of biofluorescent fish and sharks. One of his most exciting discoveries is a biofluorescent sea turtle—the first ever seen. Gruber was diving off the coast of the Solomon Islands, a nation made up of hundreds of islands in the South Pacific, during a full moon. He was using special, ultrabright blue LEDs to produce a light-up response in any bioluminescent creatures he might encounter. He was shocked when a critically endangered hawksbill sea turtle swam in front of his lights, glowing neon green and red!

Gruber needed blue light to reveal this turtle's fluorescence, but other hawksbills can see it just fine. "The sea turtles have little colored oil droplets behind their eyes," Gruber explains. Those droplets act as color filters. "So the way that a human sees the ocean is nowhere near how a sea turtle sees the ocean."

That's important, because understanding how the turtles' vision works and how they move through their environment could help people to save them. Humans could design fishing gear that the turtles would be likely to avoid. People could also design beach lights that wouldn't interfere with sea turtles' mating and their egg-laying. Gruber says, "Seeing through their eyes can teach us to interact with these creatures in a much gentler fashion."

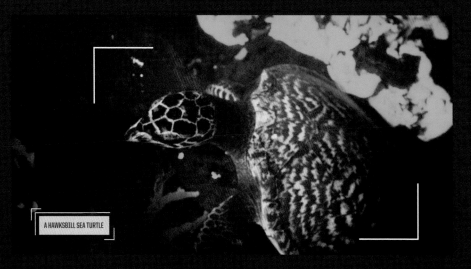

A HAWKSBILL SEA TURTLE

AMAZING REAL-LIFE UNIFORM TECHNOLOGY

Glowing jackets and the science behind them are amazing, but you don't have to be at the Academy to get a uniform that stands *way* out. In fact, there are some eye-popping uniform materials being created right now! Try these on for size.

HAGFISH-GENERATED SLIME

The snake-like hagfish defends against predators by releasing superstrong slime. The moment the slime hits water, it expands up to 10,000 times in volume, which can suffocate enemies such as sharks. The slime looks like mucus but is so strong that it's being studied as a potential material for ultralight body armor and as a way to stop enemy vessels. How can this be done? When dried, the fibers that make up the slime become stretchy thread. But uniform slime probably won't come from hagfish, which are hard to breed. Most likely, scientists would create synthetic slime.

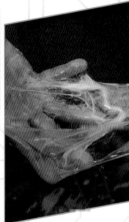

SEE-THROUGH ARMOR

Remember when Fanchon pours acid onto her feet to show she's wearing invisible, acid-resistant boots? "Transparent armor" is made of clear plastics. You can rub it with sandpaper and it won't scratch, and it can take a bullet with minimal damage. If it is dented, it can be repaired: When heated to 212°F (100°C), the "crystalline domains" it is made of pull right back into shape.

DRAGON SILK

It's tougher than steel ... much stretchier than Kevlar, the material used for bulletproof vests ... and it might make the world's strongest underwear. It's Dragon Silk! But it doesn't come from dragons. It's made by introducing spider DNA to silkworm eggs, yielding silkworms and silkworm moths that produce uniquely strong silk. This powerful thread is also soft and flexible, which is why it might make excellent military underpants.

BULLET-SMASHING FOAM

Composite metal foams (CMFs) are made of metal with tiny holes in it. The idea is similar to that of bubble wrap or Styrofoam: CMFs use air pockets to cushion impact. That's what allows them to absorb huge amounts of energy, like that from a flying bullet. Inventor Afsaneh Rabiei has suggested it could work not only for body armor but also for car bumpers.

SMART UNIFORMS

Smart uniforms come loaded with sensors that measure vital signs, sleep, steps taken, and location. They also sense the environment and can pick up traces of chemicals, bacteria, or radiation. That could have been handy for Cruz when Nebula meddled with his duffel bag in Book 4: *The Star Dunes*. A smart uniform could have sensed trouble before Cruz did.

SMART GLASSES [MIND-CONTROL CAMERA]

HOW IT WORKS AT THE ACADEMY

Your hands quiver with excitement as you put on a thin metal headband that has one lens. It's a mind-control camera! Professor Benedict explains that all you have to do is think the word "photo," look at your subject, and close your eyes for two seconds to take a picture. You turn to a pink flower on the windowsill and think, *Zoom in*. The bloom zooms close to you! Then you snap a photo. It's ready and waiting for you on your tablet.

Cruz gets back from vacation just in time to leap on board the minisub *Ridley* and join a coral reef mission in Book 5: *The Tiger's Nest*. He and his team have been assigned to photograph sea life using their mind-control cameras, which are synced with *Orion's* computer. The computer will automatically identify every image they capture ... unless they discover a new species! But Cruz forgets about his camera once aquatics instructor Jaz invites him to take the sub's pilot's seat. If he had remembered to snap some shots, they would have shown a narrow opening in a reef, surrounded by two walls of jagged coral that Cruz navigated through with white knuckles! It was probably a good idea to skip the camera there—no one wants their pilot closing his eyes, even to take an epic underwater shot.

HOW IT WORKS IN REAL LIFE

You really can take photos using mind control ... well, almost. Though not sold directly to consumers, smart glasses like Google Glass are wearable computers that look like eyeglasses with a single lens. Put them on, glance to the side, and you'll see a computer display that's controlled by voice command. An app called Winky allowed Google Glass users to take pictures by winking. Just like in the book, tightly closing an eye triggered a sensor in Google Glass to snap a pic!

Today, you might not see smart glasses on the street for a couple of reasons. One, people worried that they could invade privacy, since folks could take pictures without anyone else knowing it. Two, a lot of users thought the glasses looked silly! But smart glasses aren't gone—Google came out with an updated version in May 2019. Now, some factory workers wear smart glasses so they can read instructions while keeping their hands free to assemble products. And soldiers can use new, 3D smart glasses equipped with panoramic cameras.

AUGMEDIX GOOGLE GLASSES HELP THIS PHYSICIAN FOCUS ON HER PATIENT.

MAYBE FEASIBLE

FEASIBLE

NOT FEASIBLE

FEASIBILITY SCALE

[MIND-CONTROL CAMERA] FEASIBILITY SCALE

REAL-LIFE MIND READING

While having a device read your thoughts might sound like fantasy, it's not so far from reality. Facebook has been developing technology to enable people to type with their minds. The method uses cortical implants (electrodes in the brain) to connect to a computer and move a cursor, hands-free. People who can't move or speak on their own may be able to use cortical implants to get their thoughts across. As the technology gets better, it might allow you to communicate with people who don't speak your language, just by picturing images. No need to figure out the word for "bathroom" in Mandarin—just imagine a bathroom, and a computer will recognize the image and produce the word for it!

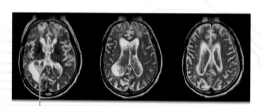

DREAM ON

In research studies, brain scanners have already been able to figure out what people are dreaming about. The scanners do it by comparing people's brain activity during sleep to their brain activity while awake. The scanners look for similarities—for instance, your brain might produce one pattern when you look at a cat, and during sleep, that pattern appears again when you dream about a cat. In a Japanese study, machines correctly guessed what people were dreaming 60 percent of the time.

THINK FAST

Scanning your brain waves could someday help you send texts and emails hands-free. "Synthetic telepathy" works by using an EEG headset. Just think about what you want to say. The headset can turn your brain wave patterns into typewritten words, then send them to a computer!

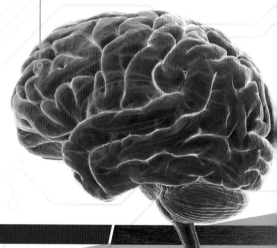

BRAIN TRAINING

Reading your thoughts can also help you train them. Biofeedback uses electrical sensors to "read" body functions such as your breathing rate, heart rate, and muscle tension so that you can learn to control them. The Muse relaxation training headband, which looks a little like Cruz's mind-control camera, uses EEG and sensory feedback to help wearers learn to control focus, anxiety, fears, and more. Muse's built-in head-phones make the sound of a storm as long as your mind is busy. When you relax and calm your thoughts, the storm settles. Talk about mind power!

A MUSE RELAXATION TRAINING HEADBAND

DIVER TECHNOLOGY
[EXPLORER ACADEMY DIVING UNIFORM]

Cruz can hardly believe his good luck in Book 2: *The Falcon's Feather* when aquatics director Tripp Scarlatos invites him to learn to pilot *Ridley*, the Academy's submersible. And even better? Tripp assigns him to a dive! Cruz is nervous, but he's got incredible underwater tech to back him up. And most of what he has is available to divers now!

LIGHTWEIGHT WET SUIT

For superstrong diving armor, pros can choose suits made from Kevlar, the same material used to make bulletproof vests. It can help guard against tears or bites, which is useful when Cruz's team is assisting whales.

SONAR RECEIVER

Sonar works by sending out a sound called a "ping," then calculating how far it went and how long it took to come back. Handheld sonar receivers can help divers find changes in depth or schools of fish. Bonus: Sonar can help you find your diving partner in murky waters or if, say, they're camouflaged with Lumagine!

ELECTROMAGNETIC SHARK DETERRENT

Shark Shield functions by emitting an electrical field. Sharks have electrical receptors in their snouts, and those sensitive receptors experience discomfort when they encounter Shark Shield's signal.

EXPLORER PROFILE: MARTINA CAPRIOTTI

During one of her first scuba dives along Italy's Adriatic Coast, Martina Capriotti spotted batteries in a natural reef where fish were grazing. Realizing how humans

were affecting the marine world, she felt she had to do something. So she started studying how garbage impacts ocean life.

"When a plastic bottle remains in the ocean for days and years, the plastics start to fragment," explains Capriotti. Once they're smaller than five millimeters (about the length of a sesame seed), they're called microplastics.

So what's the big deal? "We know microplastics can enter the digestive tract of marine animals, and in some cases, provoke injuries inside the intestines or carry a lot of contaminants (toxic molecules) on their surface," says Capriotti. Capriotti says microplastics are also showing up in human poop, proving that we're getting them through our food.

Fortunately, there are things we all can do to keep microplastics out of the water. One is to think twice before choosing single-use plastic items like bottles, straws, cups, and products with lots of packaging. And when you go shopping, remember to bring your reusable bags.

"We now are subjected to the pollution of years ago," says Capriotti. "But we can work on our future."

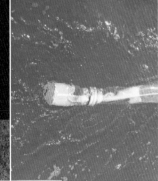

"MANTA," A SPECIAL NET, DRAGS THROUGH THE OCEAN TO COLLECT MICROPLASTICS.

ULTRA UNIFORMS: REAL-LIFE EXPLORERS' WEARABLE TECH

What would Cruz and his fellow recruits wear to explore a volcano? How about for spelunking in a cave? They'd probably take a tip from these National Geographic explorers, who have the best uniforms for extreme situations.

MARINA ELLIOTT : CAVING TECH

Marina Elliott plunges deep into the Earth to find fossil remains that tell the history of humans. She's a paleoanthropologist, which means she studies human fossils. When uncovering the bones of our ancient relatives, she dresses for the job. That could mean a helmet with a headlamp, a harness to take her up steep rock ridges, and overalls if it's warm—or a waterproof caving suit if it's cold. If there are bees in the cave entrance, she'll don a beekeeper's hat and long gloves. Additionally, she has a mask to guard against any infectious cave fungus. But for excavating, she also uses some low-tech tools ... like porcupine quills. She says, "They are sharp, but they don't scratch the fossils!"

CARSTEN PETER : *FIRE SUIT*

Carsten Peter is an adventure photographer, which means he's snapped shots deep inside caves, chased tornadoes, and even climbed into active volcanoes. So what does he wear while dodging falling rock and poisonous gases? A silvery, aluminum-treated "fire proximity suit" covers him from head to toe and reflects more than 90 percent of the radiant heat from a fire. A hood with a gold-covered window in it reflects the radiant heat and lets Peter see out. Some suits can protect against radiant heat of 3000°F (1649°C). That's hot enough to liquefy steel!

M JACKSON :
ICE CLIMBING GEAR

When Cruz and his team were chronicling glacial melt in Iceland, an island nation in Northern Europe, they were following in the footsteps of explorers like M Jackson. She specializes in studying how global warming has changed Icelandic people and their communities. When she's braving powerful winds off the ice-crusted ocean, she wears a 900-fill down jacket (that's about the most feather-packed a jacket can be!) plus at least three extra layers, waterproof gloves, water-resistant pants, wool socks (she brings along several backup pairs), a wool cap, and a helmet ... plus a harness and crampons (spiked plates that attach to the bottoms of shoes for better traction on ice). "Most importantly," says Jackson, "my outermost jacket has to have a large chest pocket where I store my smartphone." Jackson uses it to take photos, videos, and voice notes, and she has to keep it in a pocket—if she kept it in her pack, whenever she opened the pack to retrieve her phone, everything inside could get wet and freeze!

TRAINING AND SURVIVAL TECH

Waves crash as your submarine lowers into the murky depths. What's that? An enormous shark is heading straight for your sub! Good thing you've got the best tech on Earth—including a superfast submersible! At Explorer Academy, training missions can be deadly without the right gadgets.

And real-life explorers need the best tech to help them out in sticky situations, too. How about underwater robotic claws, a suit that can double your strength, or a video-equipped, mechanical worm that wriggles into tiny spaces?

Read on to learn about the awe-inspiring technology that Cruz and his fellow recruits use to solve problems and protect themselves, and the equally incredible gizmos that exist today.

A ROBOTIC UNDERWATER CAMERA

ARTIFACT ANALYZER
[PANDA UNIT: PORTABLE ARTIFACT NOTATION AND DATA ANALYZER]

HOW IT WORKS AT THE ACADEMY

In Book 3: *The Double Helix*, Cruz's teammate Dugan Marsh hits the floor when a saber-toothed cat, *Smilodon*, bounds into his class-room! He watches as the lion-size cat with foot-long teeth springs at Bryndis. She screams … and it passes right through her. It's a hologram!

Dugan realizes the whole experience was projected by a PANDA unit, an artifact analyzer that can scan an object and reveal its origin, type, and age. It can also analyze any plant or animal DNA it finds on an artifact. Dugan scanned a coprolite, otherwise known as fossilized poop. And a moment later … *Roooooaaaaar!*

If Dugan had known that a scary big cat was going to appear, he might have shut down the program before the hologram terrorized the class. *Smilodon* went extinct about 10,000 years ago, but when a PANDA unit picks up DNA, it shows what the life-form was doing shortly before its death. This one was engaged in vicious battle!

HOW IT WORKS IN REAL LIFE

The PANDA unit doesn't exist yet, but portable artifact testers do. Archaeologists like Cruz's Aunt Marisol could use these analyzers in the field or in the lab to help figure out what something is, how old it is, and where it came from.

Yet some artifacts hide information on the inside. In 2014, archaeologists discovered a 1,300-year-old, extremely delicate silver sheet rolled up inside an amulet in Jordan—trying to unroll it would have destroyed it. So, experts paired CT scanning (a type of x-ray) with 3D modeling on a computer. They were able to see inside the scroll, where they found "magical signs."

And what about writing or artwork that's painted over or blotted out? The Dead Sea Scrolls, some of the world's oldest biblical manuscripts, turned black from water exposure. Enter multispectral imaging. It works by taking photos of an artifact at different light wavelengths.

ADVANCED MULTISPECTRAL IMAGING TECHNOLOGY BEING USED TO READ BLACKENED DEAD SEA SCROLLS

Using this technique, researchers at the Israel Antiquities Authority have been able to take clear photos of the scrolls' text. "In the near infrared wavelength, you can see what the eye cannot see," explains Pnina Shor, curator and head of the Dead Sea Scrolls projects.

MAYBE FEASIBLE

NOT FEASIBLE

FEASIBLE

FEASIBILITY SCALE

[PANDA UNIT] FEASIBILITY SCALE

MOST JAW-DROPPING FINDS OF ALL TIME

Some of the world's most famous archaeological discoveries of all time took decades of work to uncover. Do you have what it takes to unearth treasures like these?

TITANIC WRECK

After colliding with an iceberg off the coast of Newfoundland in 1912, the luxury ocean liner *Titanic* seemed to vanish. In the early 1980s, National Geographic Explorer and oceanographer Robert Ballard developed Argo, a robotic underwater camera, to study sunken U.S. nuclear submarines. Argo revealed that the heaviest pieces of the subs' wreckage left a debris trail that followed ocean currents. This clue led Ballard to *Titanic*'s debris trail ... and straight to the long-lost wreck!

MACHU PICCHU

Archaeologist Hiram Bingham traveled to the Andes mountain range in 1911, searching for a secret "lost city of the Incas." He and a team of explorers hacked through jungle, crawled across a bridge made with vines, and steered clear of vipers, but it was talking to locals that brought a breakthrough. A farmer told Bingham about ruins atop a nearby mountain called Machu Picchu. There, Bingham found a stone city that had been unchanged since the 1400s!

KING TUT'S TOMB

By the 1920s, most experts were convinced there were no more undiscovered tombs hidden in Egypt's Valley of the Kings. But archaeologist Howard Carter believed there was one left. Many people said he was on a wild goose chase, yet Carter dug for years. Just before he gave up, an Egyptian boy assisting Carter's excavation team uncovered a stone slab. It was the first step down to Tut's gold-filled tomb! Tut is now one of the world's most famous Egyptian pharaohs.

TERRA-COTTA ARMY

In 1974, farmers in Xi'an, China, were trying to dig a well when their shovels hit something: life-size clay statues of warriors complete with weapons, horses, and chariots! Archaeologist Zhao Kangmin was called, and he helped to identify them as a terra-cotta army that had been buried around 200 B.C. to symbolically protect China's first emperor. Visitors can see a few thousand warriors in all!

For underwater discoveries, see page 46.

1209 0567.18

SPACE ARCHAEOLOGY

Dr. Luben is Explorer Academy's resident space archaeologist. No, he doesn't look for artifacts on other planets. Instead, he uses satellites to find archaeological sites on *our* planet. Satellite images called "tiles" can give a sky-high view of archaeological sites that haven't yet been discovered from the ground.

Cruz and his teammates get to search satellite images for signs of looting. And you can, too, by grabbing a parent and logging on to GlobalXplorer.org, a website created by real-life space archaeologist and National Geographic Explorer Sarah Parcak.

Why is it so important to stop looters? According to GlobalXplorer, more than 10,000 looted artifacts are illegally sold each day. That means those artifacts can't be properly analyzed by experts, and they may be permanently damaged.

BECOME A SPACE ARCHAEOLOGIST AT GLOBALXPLORER.ORG!

Space archaeologists look for three things to identify looter activity: shape, color, and size.

> **SHAPE:** Groups of perfectly round shapes could be pits dug by looters. Long lines could be bulldozer tracks.

> **COLOR:** Pits appear dark and stand out in images.

> **SIZE:** Most pits are seven to thirteen feet (2 to 4 m) wide. You can use the scale bar at the bottom of each image to measure them.

SARAH PARCAK USING GLOBALXPLORER.ORG

MORE MYSTERIOUS FINDS

Archaeologists sometimes uncover things that they can't explain. Can you guess why ancient civilizations created these?

COSTA RICAN STONE SPHERES

What we know: They're called Las Bolas, which means "The Balls." There are about 300 of them, and they were carved by Chibchan-speaking peoples. They might have been made to represent planets. One thing is for sure: They inspired the enormous rolling stone ball in the first Indiana Jones movie!

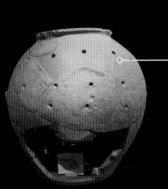

NASCA LINES OF PERU

What we know: Hundreds of these lines crisscross Peru, but they're only fully visible from the air! They look like geometric shapes, animals, and plants, and they're about 2,000 years old. The gargantuan lines might have been part of religious rituals to bring rain. Ironically, so little rain comes to that area that they've lasted for millennia.

THE KHATT SHEBIB WALL IN JORDAN

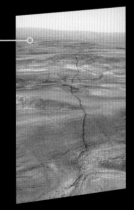

What we know: It's 93 miles (150 km) long and stood only about three feet (0.9 m) high. It might have been built as a border between farms, a watch post, a temporary shelter, or hunters' blinds. Or how about a really long balance beam?

ANCIENT ROMAN JAR FILLED WITH HOLES

What we know: It's about 1,800 years old, it's pottery, and it's full of holes. It might have been a snake jar, a mouse cage, or a lamp. So far, all the theories have holes in them.

SUBMERSIBLES [RIDLEY]

HOW IT WORKS AT THE ACADEMY

You jog down below decks on *Orion* until you see a door marked AQUATICS. You walk through, then follow a hallway to a room where you find an enormous, olive green egg. It's *Ridley*, the ship's mini submarine! You're not surprised by its shape and color. After all, it was named after an animal that looks a little like it: the Kemp's ridley, one of the most endangered sea turtles on Earth. Suddenly, the sub's four robotic arms reach out like claws. Then the top hatch slides open. Out pops your aquatics instructor, inviting you inside for a dive!

HOW IT WORKS IN REAL LIFE

Ridley **was inspired by actual submersibles.
Here are three of those gadget-filled subs**.

Bathyscaphe *Trieste*

The word "bathys" means "deep"—and that's
no understatement. The bathyscaphe *Trieste*'s thick steel cabin could handle water
pressure that would crush an ordinary submarine. In 1960, piloted by oceanographer Jacques Piccard and Lt. Don Walsh, *Trieste* dove seven miles (11 km) into the
Mariana Trench, becoming the first vessel to explore Challenger Deep, the deepest known spot in the ocean! There, Piccard and Walsh saw shrimp and fish, proving
that life exists at that depth.

DEEPSEA CHALLENGER

Trieste's achievement was matched in 2012—and with a much faster descent—when
famous film director and National Geographic Explorer James Cameron dove solo
to Challenger Deep in his "vertical torpedo" sub. Besides having a robotic claw, the
sub was tricked out with a sediment sampler to test the
ocean floor, a "slurp gun" to suck up sea creatures so
scientists could observe them, and 3D video cameras,
so you might someday be able to take a virtual
Challenger Deep dive in a real-life CAVE!

Human Occupied Vehicle *Alvin*

Alvin was made to be the ultimate vessel for
underwater study. Like *Ridley*, it has two
robotic arms that can pick up samples from the
seafloor, plus an onboard science workspace
called the "basket." Two scientists can ride at a
time, with virtual support from a team on a boat
similar to *Orion*.

RIDLEY FEATURES:

> Four robotic arms
> Six high-definition cameras
> Space for one pilot, one copilot, and eight
  passengers
> Separate back section for dive team to go out
> Travels up to 25 miles an hour (40 km/h)
> Dives almost seven miles (11 km) into the deepest
  part of the ocean

MAYBE FEASIBLE

NOT FEASIBLE

FEASIBLE

FEASIBILITY SCALE

[*RIDLEY*] FEASIBILITY SCALE

AMAZING UNDERWATER DISCOVERIES

A whopping 71 percent of our planet is covered in water. That means there's a lot of room for shipwrecks, treasure, and the remains of ancient civilizations to hide! Here are some incredible things explorers have found in the ocean.

BLACK SEA SHIPWRECK

Hanging out underwater for 2,400 years didn't destroy this ancient Greek wooden boat because the Black Sea, where it was found, has a special quality. Below 600 feet (183 m), the environment is "anoxic," which means it contains no oxygen. This condition kept the ship's wood from decaying.

3,000-YEAR-OLD TURKISH FORTRESS

A team of archaeologists and divers had been told by experts that there was nothing special beneath Lake Van in Turkey. But the team had heard local rumors of ancient ruins. And, like Cruz after he discovers a clue, they couldn't resist seeing for themselves. They persisted and found a 3,000-year-old underwater fortress! The explorers believe the ruins were gradually submerged as the lake's level rose.

WORLD'S LARGEST UNDERWATER CAVES

In Book 3: *The Double Helix*, Cruz becomes trapped in a massive underwater cave filled with artifacts—a lot like one that was found in Yucatán, Mexico. This real-life cave is a record 215 miles (346 km) long! The cave boasts the remains of 15,000-year-old giant sloths, some ancestors of elephants called gomphotheres, and lots of artifacts.

EXPLORER PROFILE: ERIKA S. BERGMAN

As a child, Erika S. Bergman wanted to find aliens. And today, that's what she does—but not in outer space. She dives into the ocean, home to some of the world's most "alien"-looking creatures.

Bergman was always interested in exploring, and while growing up, she ventured into Hawaiian jungles (like Cruz!), made fun discoveries on the Florida beaches where she played, and visited foreign cities. But it was the sea that really drew her in.

"The majority of the ocean hasn't been explored at all," Bergman says. That led her to pilot and even design her own submersible, which is how she's gotten to see amazing creatures and underwater landscapes (including shipwrecks!) that few other people have experienced.

One unglamorous discovery she's made is seeing how much junk is in the ocean. "You've heard about sea turtles with plastic wrapped around their necks," says Bergman. "The same thing can happen to a submarine." Plus, if we fill oceans with garbage, it will eventually come up to choke us on land.

That's one reason Bergman says now is the perfect time to become an underwater explorer. The more humans become aware of the incredible underwater world, the more they'll want to protect it. "There's this general sense that everything's been discovered, and it's just not true," says Bergman. In fact, exploring underwater might just help change life on land.

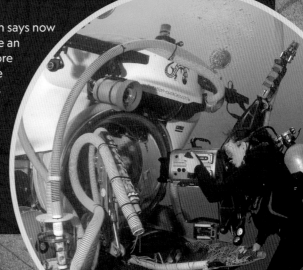

ANIMAL COMMUNICATORS
[UCC HELMET: UNIVERSAL CETACEAN COMMUNICATOR]

HOW IT WORKS AT THE ACADEMY

You feel the spray as a pod of dolphins leaps and splashes in the ocean. It's almost as if they want you to come play. And you're about to get the chance to ask them! You pull a shiny, black dive helmet over your head. It's an Universal Cetacean Communicator (UCC for short). All you need to do now is swim within 20 feet (6.1 m) of a cetacean (that's a whale, dolphin, or porpoise), and start talking. The helmet will translate your words so that the animals can understand!

When Cruz puts on the UCC in Book 2: *The Falcon's Feather*, he has a serious mission. He needs to talk to and soothe a school of whales trapped in fishing gear. Though the creatures are 10 times his body length and could kill him with a nudge, as soon as Cruz starts explaining he's come to help, they become calm. They stay still while members of Cruz's team work to set them free. And when their low sounds are translated through the helmet, Cruz is moved to hear what they've said: "Joy."

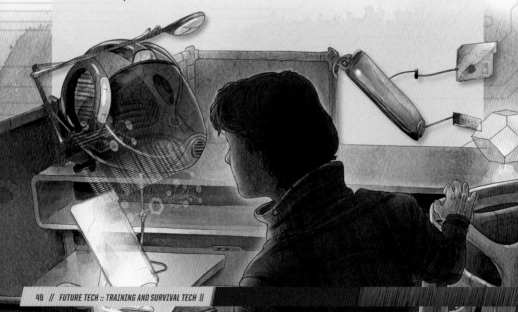

HOW IT WORKS IN REAL LIFE

The UCC translates human language into cetacean-speak, but in the book, the animals don't speak in sentences. Instead, they use sounds that express what they're feeling or thinking, like *tired* or *help*. And though there's no UCC in real life, researchers are finding that the language of cetaceans works in a similar way.

A SCIENTIST LISTENING TO HYDROPHONE RECORDINGS

"Whale song" is the low series of tones that whales make. Experts use hydrophones, which are underwater microphones, to record cetaceans' sounds. They've found that killer whales have signature calls for themselves— what we might think of as their names! And National Geographic Explorers David Gruber and Robert Wood are co-developing a small device that will help divers record whales' calls.

There's also a dolphin communicator designed by Dr. Thad Starner and his team at Georgia Tech. It's called CHAT, which stands for "Cetacean Hearing and Telemetry," and it's a wearable translation device. When researchers wore it near a pod of dolphins they'd been training, it captured a whistle the team had previously taught the dolphins to recognize as "seaweed." The CHAT played it back in English! But that's still far from translating dolphins' natural language into human language. For now, it proves that dolphins can learn language we teach them, and they can try to communicate with us.

MAYBE FEASIBLE

NOT FEASIBLE

FEASIBLE

FEASIBILITY SCALE

[UCC HELMET] FEASIBILITY SCALE

EXPLORER PROFILE: BRIAN SKERRY

Growing up in Massachusetts, Brian Skerry loved going to the beach. "The ocean represented this really cool place to me, that spoke to me of discovery," he says. "My parents put in a pool when I was three, and I'd put on a mask and fins and pretend I was diving with animals." Then, as a teenager, he saw a presentation of work by underwater photographers and filmmakers, and he realized that was what he wanted to do. "My ultimate goal was to work for National Geographic," Skerry says. To achieve his goals, he studied diving, filmmaking, and photography—and it paid off! Today, he's an underwater photographer who dives with dolphins, sharks, and other sea life to create photo features for *National Geographic* magazine. One of his shark photos is among National Geographic's "Fifty Greatest Photos of All Time."

Skerry says he hopes his photos will inspire people to help save the ocean and all that lives in it. "We've taken 90 percent of the fish from the ocean," says Skerry. "More than half of the world's coral reefs have been destroyed. We're dumping so much carbon into the atmosphere, the ocean is becoming acidic, and that's further eroding anything with a seashell." His aim is for people to remember his photos, and to be moved to create solutions.

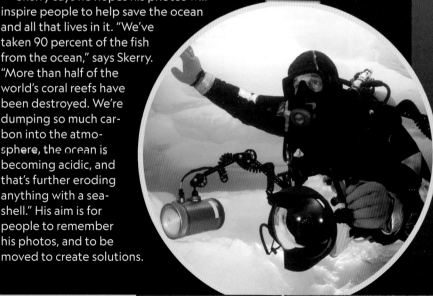

CETACEAN COMMUNICATION CHEAT SHEET

As Brian Skerry learned while working on a cover story about dolphin intelligence, dolphins are some of the most conversational cetaceans. Because they see their world mostly through sound and use acoustics to hunt with their pod, or group, dolphins have a complex language that they use to communicate with one another. They make three main types of sounds: clicks, whistles, and "burst-pulse" sounds. Can you learn to speak dolphin? Here's what researchers have figured out so far.

CLICKS

Clicks are what our ears hear, but they can be combined with ultrasonic sounds that we *can't* hear. The clicks bounce off objects and come back to the dolphins in what's called echo-location. The sounds tell dolphins, "There's something out there, and I can tell how big it is and how far away."

WHISTLES

These can sound like high-pitched squeals, and they're the main way dolphins "talk." An urgent whistle from a dolphin calf can mean, "Mom! Where are you?" Rising and falling whistles might mean, "Hey! This is fun." And a whistle unlike any other could be the dolphin saying its name!

BURST-PULSE

To human ears, these sound like squawks or barks, but they're actually very fast clicks. Fighting dolphins may use them to say, "Watch out! I'm tough!"

CRITTER CHAT
MORE ANIMAL COMMUNICATION

As handy as the UCC would be underwater, most of us would first like to figure out what the animals in our own homes have to say. If you wish your pet could hold up its end of the conversation, you're in luck—researchers are learning how to tell what all kinds of animals are communicating, and you don't need a UCC to translate.

CATS AND DOGS

Cats and dogs aren't the best candidates for a voice recognition device. That's because they do a lot of their "talking" through movement. A cat's tail, ear, eye, and even whisker positions can communicate her mood, from loving to angry. Narrow, slowly blinking eyes mean "I love you"; a wagging tail means "I'm mad!" And what about when your cat opens her mouth, but no sound comes out? Some researchers suggest that the cat is meowing at a higher pitch than humans can hear, possibly to say, "I'm hungry!"

As for dogs, you already know that Hubbard's wagging tail means he's happy. But did you know the speed of the wag matters? A slow wag could mean he's unsure or feeling a little worried. And while yawning often means he's tired, it can also mean he's stressed. But if you ever hear a dog make a huffing sound during play, that's a reason to smile. Some experts say that's a dog's laugh!

PRAIRIE DOGS

These relatives to pet rodents have a lot to say. Researcher Con Slobodchikoff is using artificial intelligence to analyze prairie dog calls, and he's figured out that prairie dogs not only have different calls for different predators, but they can also describe humans they've met. Prairie dogs use chirps to specify people's size and shape, what color they're wearing, and even what they're carrying!

FISH

If you're a fish owner, you've probably tried to talk to your scaly friends. And studies suggest that some fish are getting the message. Archerfish hunt by spitting water at bugs to knock them off branches. Researchers showed archerfish pictures of faces, and rewarded them when they spat at familiar faces among dozens of unfamiliar ones. The fish did so with up to 86 percent accuracy. Now, when the study's co-author enters the lab, the fish spits in her eye. Could that be her fish saying "Hi"?

ANIMAL VENOMS [OCTOPOD]

HOW IT WORKS AT THE ACADEMY

You hold a pinball-size black ball in your hand, being careful not to press any of the blue rings that cover it. It's called an octopod, and although it looks like a cool toy, Fanchon explained that this gadget is actually a defensive tool. One press on a blue ring and it releases a paralyzing spray! The spray is made with deadly venom from the tiny blue-ringed octopus. If you're ever cornered in a dark alley, a spritz from the octopod won't kill your attacker, but it will stop her or him for 15 minutes, leaving time for you to escape!

Cruz needs to use the octopod for real on Halloween night in Book 3: *The Double Helix*. During a party in the CAVE, Cruz is blindfolded, playing a "mystery box" game in which he reaches into a box and has to guess the items he feels. While he's guessing, a Nebula agent appears behind him and demands the pieces of his mother's cipher! A hand wraps around his throat. Cruz jabs his elbow into the attacker, then spins around and sprays the octopod. The peacock blue mist works! Cruz gets away, at least for now ...

[OCTOPOD] FEASIBILITY SCALE

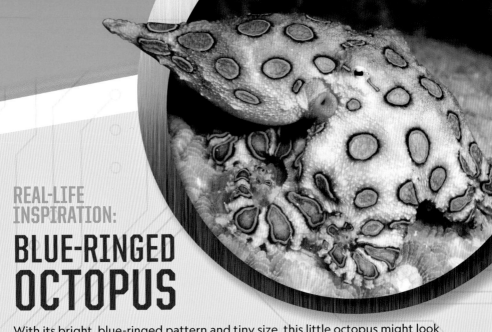

REAL-LIFE INSPIRATION:

BLUE-RINGED OCTOPUS

With its bright, blue-ringed pattern and tiny size, this little octopus might look adorable. But watch out—it's an ultra-venomous killer!

Found in Pacific Ocean tide pools and coral reefs, there are at least 10 species of blue-ringed octopuses. To potential predators, the octopus's rings are a warning to stay back. After all, the animal's venom is powerful enough to kill 26 humans within minutes! Its killer substance is called tetrodotoxin, and it's produced by bacteria in the octopus's salivary glands.

The octopod has a beak that works as a sprayer, but the real creature uses its beak to peck into animals and insert its venom. While hunting, the blue-ringed octopus pecks to paralyze sea creatures and quickly turn them into a seafood buffet. It can also release a cloud of ultra-powerful venom into the water that seeps into potential prey through their gills.

What's most dangerous about this octopus is that its bite isn't always felt. So keep your eyes open because it will give you a warning. Whenever the octopus is agitated, its rings light up like the octopod's!

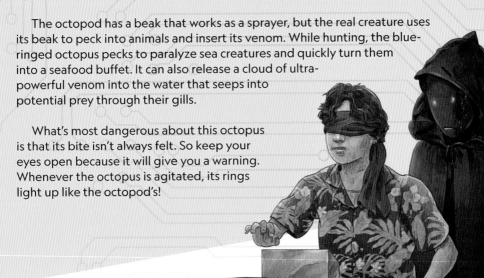

ANIMAL VENOMS

EXPLORER PROFILE: ZOLTAN TAKACS

Like Cruz's mom, Zoltan Takacs studies animal venoms and how they can help humans. He started catching snakes as a boy. Later, he was amazed to learn that even though some of the world's top lifesaving

medications come from snake venoms, as many as 20 million venoms still haven't been studied. That's why Takacs is building disease-focused toxin libraries that may one day result in novel therapy. And he does this despite the fact that he's allergic to both snake venom and antivenom! So how does he stay safe? When he finds a venomous snake, he holds it in place with a long stick, then leads it into a transparent tube, so it can't bite him while he's working. He takes a tiny tissue sample, the genetic blueprint of toxins, to add to his toxin library, then typically sets the snake free, always steering clear of fangs.

Takacs also collects toxins from Gila monsters, sea anemones, scorpions, and other venomous animals. Scary as that sounds, even more dangerous are the places these animals live. Takacs has survived jungle swamps and desert storms, and he's narrowly avoided charging elephants and hungry crocodiles. Takacs feels it's worth the risk because someday the toxins he collects may stop diseases like multiple sclerosis, rheumatoid arthritis, and cancer. He hopes that humans will realize how valuable these "scary" animals are and learn to respect them and their habitat.

LIFESAVING VENOMS

The blue-ringed octopus may be a killer, but some venoms, as Zoltan Takacs has come to find, have as much power to help as they do to hurt.

Captopril is a tablet used to protect the heart, treat high blood pressure, and even boost chances of survival following a heart attack. Most people who take captopril probably don't know its powers are from Brazilian viper venom! The venom blocks an enzyme that constricts blood vessels, making it easier for the heart to pump blood through the body. Today, captopril is made as a synthetic compound that mimics the venom toxin.

Another serpent worth researching is the black mamba, an African snake dubbed the world's deadliest because untreated bites have very high fatality rates. However, its venom contains a toxin that could potentially serve as a painkiller that might help people recover from serious injuries.

And the paralyzing, predatory cone snail is already helping people. Like the black mamba, it has a component in its venom that works as a painkiller. This one is up to *10,000* times stronger than the painkiller generally used in hospitals. Ziconotide is a medicine that uses a synthetic version of cone snail venom toxin to block pain signals from reaching the brain.

A BLACK MAMBA REARS UP.

WILD INVENTIONS

FUTURISTIC TECH INSPIRED BY ANIMALS

When it comes to cool animal-inspired gadgets, the octopod has some competition. Here are some impressive human take-offs on the wild world.

SHARKSKIN BOAT COATING

The U.S. Navy has a problem with barnacles and other marine life sticking to its ships. Barnacles can slow down a vessel, which costs lots of money in fuel, and removing them can cost millions. But sharks don't get barnacles. Why? Their scales each have spines that make it hard for creatures to latch on. So researchers have developed a synthetic sharkskin coating made of silicone for the outside of ships. It reduces barnacles by up to 67 percent!

SPINY-HEADED WORM-INSPIRED SKIN GRAFTS

A successful study led to an invention. When surgeons need to attach lifesaving skin grafts (pieces of healthy skin transplanted to wounded parts of the body), they copy a spiny-headed worm. This worm pokes its sharp spine into its host, then its head inflates to stay in place. A worm-inspired skin graft adhesive uses "microneedles" whose tips swell when they become moist inside the body, just as the worm does. It makes the graft more than three times stronger than surgical staples, with less risk of infection.

SOFT ROBOTICS INSPIRED BY CAT TONGUES

The rough spines on a cat's tongue serve to grab and brush kitty fur, then rotate when they hit a snag. Researchers have 3D-printed a plastic cat tongue to study how its soft spines could help soft robotics (robots that can bend and squish—read more on page 72) get a similarly strong, flexible grip. This same spiny quality could also be built into the design of a new hairbrush for people!

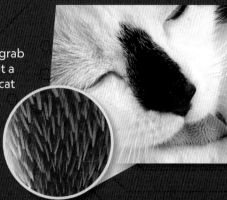

JELLYFISH SKIN TO STOP SMARTPHONE GLARE

Ever look at a smartphone screen and see the sun instead of the display? That's glare. Jellyfish might have a way of stopping this pesky glare. When some types of jellyfish get scared, their skin forms a wrinkled surface. As it turns out, those "micro-wrinkles" scatter light instead of reflecting it as glare. Scientists are trying to copy this effect for phones.

LONG-NOSED BULLET TRAINS INSPIRED BY KINGFISHERS

When Japanese bullet trains were first invented, they had a problem. When a bullet train left a tunnel, traveling at 200 miles an hour (321.9 km/h), air molecules built up at the train's nose and exploded, causing a deafening sound called a sonic boom. To reduce the noise, engineers copied the kingfisher, a bird with a long, pointed beak that doesn't make a splash as it hurtles nose first into the water. The water slides along the bird's beak instead of being pushed ahead. Now, bullet trains have long noses, mimicking the kingfisher's beak, and they are much quieter.

A BULLET TRAIN SPEEDS THROUGH JAPAN.

ANIMALS TEACHING SCIENTISTS

As impressive as they are, octopods' defense mechanisms aren't as complex as those of real octopuses, and even the best UCC can't measure up to a cetacean's complex voice. In fact, animals are outsmarting our best technology every day, and scientists are racing to keep up!

ANIMAL ALARM

In 2011 in Peru, a country in western South America, there was a magnitude 7 earthquake. Three weeks before the quake, animals began to clear out of Yanachaga National Park. Yet scientists started observing seismic activity only two weeks before the quake. Similar events have been reported throughout the world, leading some scientists to think that the animals were tipped off by electromagnetic radiation from the ground. Figuring out how that animal intuition works may one day help save humans, too.

In Sicily, Italy, farm animals have been outsmarting a different kind of natural disaster. Between 2012 and 2014, goats and sheep appear to have known when an active volcano would erupt before humans knew it. Four to six hours before Mount Etna erupted, the animals woke in the middle of the night and started walking. By daylight, they had moved to a different area. When the eruption occurred, the animals were safe. Scientists have begun tagging farm animals with a kind of fitness tracker, hoping they'll act like an early disaster warning system for humans.

A SCIENTIST TRACKS A TAGGED FARM ANIMAL.

BOWHEAD WHALES LIVE
IN ARCTIC WATERS.

NICE GENES

Marine animals may help save humans in
another dramatic way. Bowhead whales can live
to be more than 200 years old. Scientists have determined that one
reason the whales live so long is that they don't get cancer. Experts
suspect that the whales have anti-tumor mechanisms built into their
genes. Researchers are now studying whales' genomes (their genetic
profile) to learn how they work.

NO SUCKER

Another creature that is helping
scientists is the bloodsucking leech,
which might be the best buddy of
ecologists fighting to conserve
remote rainforests. The leeches
carry DNA from all the dead animals they feed on, so scientists
can check a single leech to learn
about mammal diversity in an
environment. This is valuable
because the more biodiversity
that conservationists find, the
more likely it is that they will be
able to convince governments that
the land deserves protection. Now
that's one wonderfully helpful
segmented worm!

LEECHES CAN BE FOUND
ALL OVER THE WORLD.

CUTTING-EDGE TECH
FOR EXPLORERS

Scientific breakthroughs are happening so fast that even Cruz and his team don't have this new, real-life tech. Consider packing these for your next futuristic mission!

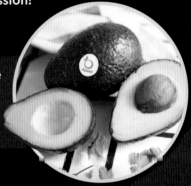

EDIPEEL

This new edible coating is made from produce peels, seeds, and pulp. It can keep moisture in your fruits and veggies while keeping oxygen out, doubling perishable snacks' shelf life (or life in your pack).

CELLPOD

This micro appliance is being developed to grow the ingredients for your meals within a week. It produces "plant cells," which are the most nutritious parts of the plant, but in cellular form. A little mushy, but tasty!

MESHWORM

This mini bot is styled after an earthworm. It can quietly creep into tiny spaces to measure temperature, record audio, and maybe even record video in future versions. Plus it's nearly indestructible. Nebula agents could stomp on it and it would just keep slithering along!

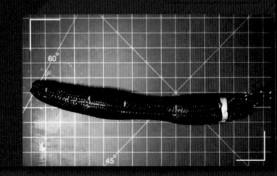

GRAVITY JET SUIT BY GRAVITY INDUSTRIES

One way to search for clues on the ground or to escape bad guys in a hurry is to strap on a jet pack. This one can fly you as high as 12,000 feet (3,658 m) for eight minutes! The only downside? It costs half a million dollars.

ONYX EXOSKELETON

Wearing this getup could double your endurance, which means you could climb, run, or lift heavy stuff twice as long as usual. Strap it to your legs, and its sensors and artificial intelligence would reduce stress and fatigue on your muscles, giving you serious superpowers. Now you're definitely ready to take on Nebula!

ANIMAL SPY CAMERAS

[SHOT-BOT (SOFT HELIOMORPHIC OBSERVATIONAL TRAVELING ROBOT)]

HOW IT WORKS AT THE ACADEMY

Fanchon's assistant, Dr. Sidril Vanderwick, presents you with what looks like a clear toaster oven waffle. You press a remote, and the "waffle" turns green and starts to stretch like slime! The slime takes the shape of a stem, leaves, and pink buds that twirl into flowers. You realize you're looking at a SHOT-bot, a camera that can disguise itself as almost any plant. It can follow and photograph wild animals without the animals knowing it!

In Book 4: *The Star Dunes*, Cruz and his team get assigned to deploy SHOT-bots in Namibia. When Cruz, Emmett, Sailor, and Dugan spot a poacher, one bot really gets a chance to shine: Dugan suggests using it to snap photos of the poachers. Just then, an endangered pangolin and its baby wander closer and closer to the dangerous poachers. Luckily, another robot—Mell!—whizzes to the rescue. With Mell's stinger in action and the SHOT-bot taping the whole thing, there's a happy ending for the pangolins—but not the poachers.

MAYBE FEASIBLE

FEASIBLE

NOT FEASIBLE

FEASIBILITY SCALE

[SHOT-BOT] FEASIBILITY SCALE

HOW IT WORKS IN REAL LIFE

A panda cub reaches for a branch ... takes a wobbly step ... then tumbles into its mama's waiting paws. It has no idea that its first steps are being recorded by a hidden camera inside its favorite food, bamboo!

While there isn't yet a robot that can turn into a plant like the SHOT-bot does, there are robotic cameras that wear disguises to film animals, and the Bamboo Cam, used in remote Chinese mountains where pandas live, is one of them. Other hidden cams can be, well, stinky. In Africa's Serengeti, a photographer placed his remote-controlled camera inside a dung ball! It captured close-ups of unsuspecting elephants, zebras, warthogs, and hippos. Less gross? A camera covered in mirrors that rolls along forest floors, making it invisible to bears who live there.

Not every spy camera is made to hide from animals. Robotic hyenas, fake crocodile babies, animatronic chimpanzees, and more animal look-alikes have been built to tempt wild animals to interact with them. Their eyes are camera lenses!

ANIMAL SPY CAMERAS / SHOT-BOT
WHY EXPLORERS WANT IT

A WORKER GETS READY TO DEPLOY A TRAILGUARD DEVICE.

The SHOT-Bot isn't the only hidden camera that can help stop bad guys. TrailGuard, an artificial intelligence–enhanced spy cam, made its debut in 2018 at Grumeti Game Reserve in Tanzania, Africa. Shortly after being deployed, one TrailGuard caught a picture of what looked like a man carrying supplies. Workers in the park's operations room saw the image and realized this was a potential poacher! Hours later, the poacher who was caught on camera and his team were found and arrested along with their stolen goods.

TrailGuard works by using an infrared sensor. Whenever someone or something crosses its path, it takes a picture. Its image recognition software analyzes the photo, and if it finds a human or a vehicle it sends rangers an alert.

This is a big deal because poaching—when people illegally catch and sell animals or their parts—is one of the biggest threats to wildlife today. More than 100,000 African elephants were killed by poachers between 2014 and 2017, and more than a thousand rhinos are poached annually for their horns.

Fortunately, TrailGuard's tech is getting more sophisticated all the time. Hopefully, poachers soon won't stand a chance.

PHOTOS CAPTURED BY TRAIL-GUARDS HELP PARK RANGERS IDENTIFY POACHERS.

THE SAFEST RHINOS ON THE PLANET

Rhinos are some of the most threatened creatures on the planet: one is killed every eight hours. Poachers are after their horns, which are as valuable as gold in some countries because some people believe that they can cure disease. (The horns are mostly just keratin, the same stuff our fingernails are made of.)

Desperate to protect these endangered animals, conservationists have tried many ways to discourage poachers. They've placed trackers in rhinos' horns or even removed horns entirely, but that means tranquilizing the animals, which is expensive and potentially dangerous for both humans and the animals.

Helping Poachers, Too

People often poach because they need money. Fortunately, would-be poachers are learning that live rhinos are very valuable: Tourists are eager to see healthy rhinos. And local residents can earn money to support their families by becoming tour guides.

So technologists came up with a new idea: Instead of tracking rhinos, why not track people? At one South African rhino reserve, wireless trackers were placed on every car and person authorized to enter. Every vehicle and person who tries to enter the park is scanned. Thermal cameras, magnetic sensors, and an alarmed, electrified fence were installed, too (Emmett Lu would be proud). And the data show it's working! In the first 18 months, poaching fell by 96 percent.

CHAPTER 3.0

EVERYDAY TECH

Imagine if instead of asking your parents for a ride, you could rent a driverless car—no adult supervision required. No need to load the trunk with stuff, because you could simply use your tablet to order essentials once you reached your destination—they'd be delivered by drone, of course. With tech like this, you could get out and go explore, anytime, anyplace.

Tech that explorers, and you, can use to make life easier may be called "everyday tech," but that doesn't mean it's ordinary. Check out some creations you could use on an everyday basis to make regular life a whole lot cooler.

ROBOBEES [MELL]

HOW IT WORKS AT THE ACADEMY

She whooshes to the ceiling and dives toward the floor, swooping upward right before impact. She slows, then makes a perfect landing in your hand. She's Mell the "Micro Air Vehicle," a bumblebee drone you can control with voice command! "Mell, test flight," you say. The insect bot blinks her golden eyes at you, signaling that she understands. Then she whizzes away to perform a figure-8 through your dorm room, and takes some video and photos. That's cool, but she *really* comes in handy when Nebula is around.

In Book 1: *The Nebula Secret*, Cruz, Sailor, and Emmett race to escape a man chasing them through the Academy. Breathless, they rush into a supply closet. The smell of pickles fills the small space. It's poison gas, and the teammates are locked inside! Their only hope is Mell, who's far away in Cruz's dorm. Before Cruz left home for the Academy, Lani programmed Mell to communicate through a honeycomb-shaped remote. She's supposed to be able to take commands from up to 4,000 feet (1,219 m) away. But will she?

HOW IT WORKS IN REAL LIFE

Mell was inspired by real micro drones built by electrical engineer and National Geographic Explorer Robert Wood. Although Wood's RoboBees don't have stingers, Wood designed the insect-size bots with the capability to one day perform rescue operations. Until recently, they could only hover or fly on a tether along simple, preprogrammed routes. But breakthroughs in powering RoboBees have made it possible to leave their tethers behind. Eventually, Wood hopes RoboBees will be able to zoom into places that would be too difficult or dangerous for humans to enter, like collapsed buildings or chemical spill sites, and help to find accident survivors or to collect lifesaving information. They won't be controlled by voice command or a joystick, and for a good reason. "They're much faster than a human mind and hand could control," explains Wood. Instead, they'll fly by themselves, using tools like heat-seeking sensors to find survivors, and preprogrammed commands to keep them from bumping into walls.

When RoboBees find what they're after, they'll wirelessly *buzz* a message.

MAYBE FEASIBLE

FEASIBLE

NOT FEASIBLE

FEASIBILITY SCALE

[MELL] FEASIBILITY SCALE

ROBOBEES

EXPLORER PROFILE: ROBERT WOOD

Like a lot of kids, Robert Wood got interested in tinkering with robots early on. "I was a curious child, making Legos and playing with

remote-controlled vehicles," says Wood. "I got my first robot when I was about five. I think my interest really picked up speed when I got to graduate school." There, Wood was studying electrical engineering when he learned about a robotics project. "It was the predecessor to the RoboBees," says Wood. He was especially interested in the fact that none of the parts for this project could be bought—every one of them had to be created from scratch. So he got to work!

Today, Wood is developing new made-from-scratch robots using materials you might not expect. "The typical robot is made of hard plastics and metals," explains Wood. Wood and his team are changing that up with what are called "soft robotics." Made from flexible, sometimes squishy materials, soft bots work better than hard ones in many situations.

For starters, soft robots can squeeze through spaces instead of going around objects. This could help with search and rescue. They can also be used as surgical instruments for internal and external procedures. "Being in close contact with a human, just for safety reasons, you might not want [a robot] to be so rigid," says Wood. In other words, they won't accidentally jab you! And there's Second Skin, a wearable prototype Wood helped develop: It detects abnormalities in the way people move and nudges the wearers to correct them!

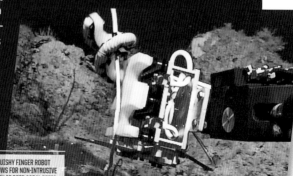

A SQUISHY FINGER ROBOT ALLOWS FOR NON-INTRUSIVE STUDY OF DEEP CORAL REEFS.

THE FUTURE OF **ROBOBEES**

RoboBees' microchip "brains" may one day be able to learn, thanks to what's called a deep neural network (DNN). Like Mell, once a RoboBee has seen something or been somewhere, it will recognize it. Deep neural networks work a little like learning to ride a bike. Every time the robot succeeds, it "remembers" that success and repeats what worked in the past. When it fails, it doesn't try that move again. The only minus: Failures can mean some broken robots!

Another possible use for RoboBees is to copy real bees. Colony collapse disorder is a phenomenon in which worker bees disappear, leaving the rest of the bee colony vulnerable to dying out. Bees pollinate almost three-quarters of the world's top 100 crops, so this disorder is a serious problem. Without bees, we could lose most of the nutrient-rich fruits and veggies we need to survive. Researchers have suggested that RoboBees could act as robotic pollinators, and programmers are teaching them to work as a colony!

RoboBees' technology can be applied to new micro robots. These robots could perform superhuman jobs, such as crawling through a jet engine and searching for faults. "We've also been exploring how micro robots can jump," says Wood. Imagine a robotic bug that could leap up a skyscraper and find a problem in its structure. Move over, Spider-Man!

THE ROBOBEE, AND ITS BIOLOGICAL COUNTERPART, PERCHING ON PLANTS

THIS NEW ROBOBEE MODEL WEIGHS ONLY 80 MILLIGRAMS.

MIND-BLOWING DRONES

Mell is a type of drone—a pilotless, remote-controlled aircraft. Drones were named after the droning sound of a male bee, and you might know them best for the aerial videos they can take. But drones can do a lot more than make impressive movies.

If you ever find yourself on a training mission where you're marooned on an island, stuck on a mountain or adrift in the ocean, the Little Ripper Lifesaver drone could fly to your rescue. In 2018, it became the first drone to rescue a surfer from stormy seas! The drone works by delivering lifesaving equipment, including rafts, thermal blankets, mobile defibrillators (devices to restart the heart), first aid kits, and food. It also has artificial intelligence and a camera to alert swimmers to nearby sharks.

A FLUIDITY TECH AVIATOR DRONE CONTROLLER

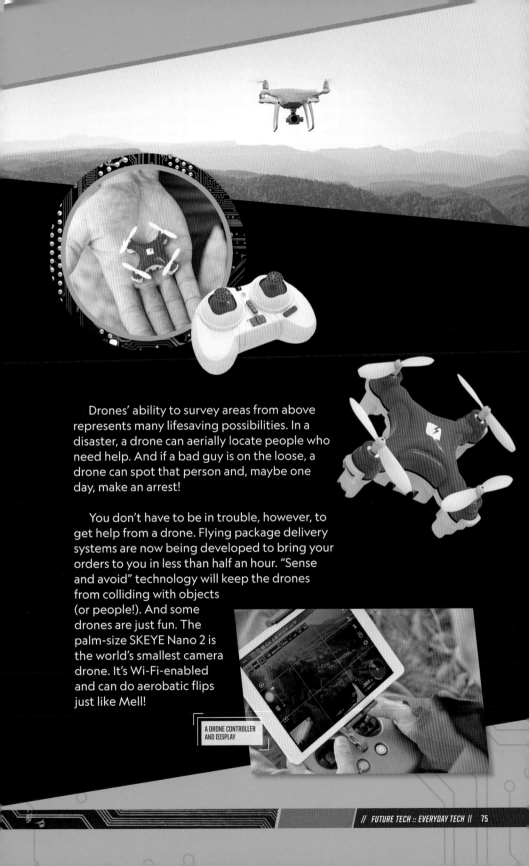

Drones' ability to survey areas from above represents many lifesaving possibilities. In a disaster, a drone can aerially locate people who need help. And if a bad guy is on the loose, a drone can spot that person and, maybe one day, make an arrest!

You don't have to be in trouble, however, to get help from a drone. Flying package delivery systems are now being developed to bring your orders to you in less than half an hour. "Sense and avoid" technology will keep the drones from colliding with objects (or people!). And some drones are just fun. The palm-size SKEYE Nano 2 is the world's smallest camera drone. It's Wi-Fi-enabled and can do aerobatic flips just like Mell!

A DRONE CONTROLLER
AND DISPLAY

TABLETS

HOW IT WORKS AT THE ACADEMY

You gingerly hold a device the thickness of a greeting card. You can hardly believe this slim gadget is loaded with a library's worth of textbooks, tons of video training sessions, all your notebooks, and, of course, email and internet. The tablet chimes, and adviser Taryn Secliff appears on your screen. "If you're getting this message, your team has been selected for an important mission," she says. "Report to the third-deck conference room immediately." Excited, you tap the screen, and a map shows you where to go!

Cruz takes his trusty tablet almost everywhere. He uses it to record clues so he can work on solving them later, to keep in touch with Aunt Marisol when he's searching for hidden cipher pieces, and to connect with his best friend, Lani, when they're far apart. But in Book 1: *The Nebula Secret*, it almost gets him kicked out of the Academy. A hacker changes the CAVE's programming to make Team Cousteau's mission easier. The hack is traced back to Cruz's tablet. It seems the tiny device is capable of affecting the CAVE's alternate-reality environment. But Cruz knows he isn't the hacker. He sets out to find the culprit to save his reputation. And luckily, explorers don't give up!

MAYBE FEASIBLE

NOT FEASIBLE

FEASIBLE

FEASIBILITY SCALE

[TABLETS] FEASIBILITY SCALE

FOLDABLE PHONE

HOW IT WORKS IN REAL LIFE

Tablets today can do incredible things, including most of what Cruz's tablet can do. They take photos, run video, and have touch screens. Some even use facial recognition. Still, they're not yet as thin as greeting cards. The thinnest tablet to date is just under a quarter of an inch (5.5 mm) thick, about as wide as three stacked nickels.

THE INSIDE OF A NANOWIRE AS VIEWED THROUGH AN ELECTRON MICROSCOPE

The trouble with superskinny tablets is that the thinner they are, the more easily they can break—a major problem for Cruz, who's dropped his more than once. But researchers have some ideas to fix that. One is ultrathin nanowires. Nanowires can be woven into a flexible material that could be used to create paper-thin devices. At only three atoms wide, these would be the skinniest wires ever made.

Foldable device prototypes are also made today, including phones that wrap around your wrist or unfold like origami. Their screens bend instead of snapping because they're made of lots of tiny pixels, not a solid sheet.

BONUS!
The cameras on future tablets may be pretty neat, too. They might use multi-lens cameras that shoot simultaneously to build one big photo, kind of how a bug's compound eye works!

SELF-DRIVING CARS

HOW IT WORKS AT THE ACADEMY

When you disembark from *Orion*, you're directed to a car with no driver. *What kind of mission is this?* you think. You don't even have a license. You get in and a computerized voice says, "Welcome to Auto Auto. Your destination is preset as Denali National Park." You realize this car drives by itself! You've always wanted to see the park's glaciers and sled dogs in Alaska. The car eases away from the curb and onto the road. You check out the sites through your GPS sunglasses, take some mind-control photos, then lean back and close your eyes. When you wake up, a chill is in the air, snow is crunching under the tires, and Denali's white peak is looming above you!

One night in Book 4: *The Star Dunes*, Cruz gets into an Auto Auto without telling anyone. He takes off for the Namibian Desert, following one of his mom's clues. But even a self-driving car isn't fail-safe. Nebula tracks Cruz's Auto Auto in a truck and nearly forces it off the road. Cruz is shaken. Though the self-driving supercar is damaged, it evaluates itself and determines it's still safe to operate. Talk about a lifesaving piece of tech!

MAYBE FEASIBLE

FEASIBLE

FEASIBILITY SCALE

[SELF-DRIVING CARS]
FEASIBILITY SCALE

NAVYA

HOW IT WORKS IN REAL LIFE

SELF-DRIVING CARS

Vroom, vroom! Get ready to ride, because self-driving cars are already here! In the near future in certain cities, you will click the app for Waymo, and a self-driving car will cruise your way. Accidents might be less likely in a self-driving car than when a human is behind the wheel: According to Waymo's creators, 94 percent of serious car crashes are caused by user error. Waymo uses sensors and software to detect other drivers, pedestrians, and objects, and it predicts their movement based on their speed and direction. Waymo cars can recognize traffic light colors, railroad crossing gates, and stop signs. In fact, they can sense up to three football fields away in all directions!

SELF-DRIVING BUSES

What if instead of putting single people in individual vehicles, we used self-driving buses? In several cities, these are on the road. Hop a ride in Navya, autonomous, electric shuttles and cabs available at airports around the world. Or in Maryland, step aboard autonomous minibus Olli and ask it to recommend a place to eat, fill you in on the weather, or tell a joke. Olli can do it all, though it can't guarantee it'll make you laugh!

DELIVERY DRONES

If you're not quite ready to step into a driverless car, you can ask one to "visit" you. Some Kroger supermarkets have started using Nuro, a little vehicle called a "rolling delivery drone." It can bring up to 20 bags of groceries to your door. Now that's service.

WAYMO

THE TECH: SELF-DRIVING CARS— HIGHWAYS OF THE FUTURE

What would a world of self-driving vehicles look like? Some experts predict that the number of deadly car crashes would fall by 90 percent. Plus, fewer people would actually own cars because they could subscribe to a car service like Auto Auto. Better yet, you wouldn't need to search for parking spots—after your car drops you off, it could park itself.

SAFE CROSSWALKS—CARS STOP AUTOMATICALLY.

NARROWER STREETS—AUTONOMOUS CARS CAN NAVIGATE WITH MORE PRECISION THAN HUMANS CAN.

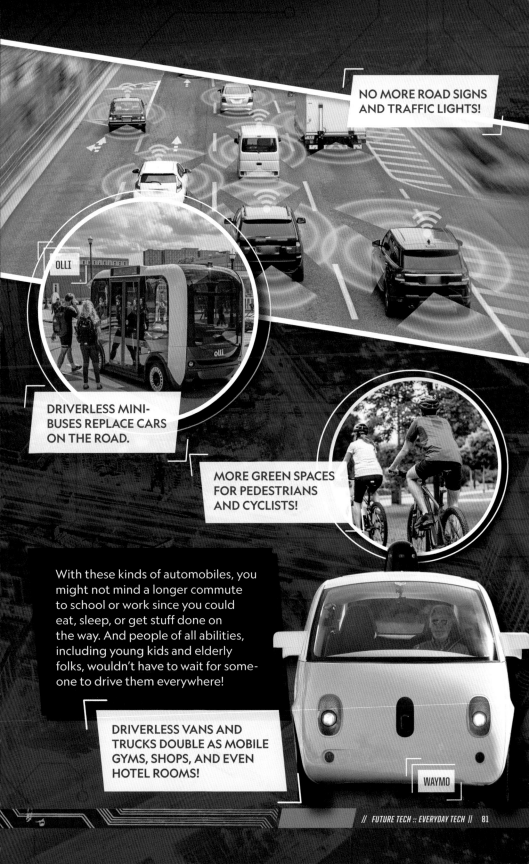

NO MORE ROAD SIGNS AND TRAFFIC LIGHTS!

OLLI

DRIVERLESS MINI-BUSES REPLACE CARS ON THE ROAD.

MORE GREEN SPACES FOR PEDESTRIANS AND CYCLISTS!

With these kinds of automobiles, you might not mind a longer commute to school or work since you could eat, sleep, or get stuff done on the way. And people of all abilities, including young kids and elderly folks, wouldn't have to wait for someone to drive them everywhere!

DRIVERLESS VANS AND TRUCKS DOUBLE AS MOBILE GYMS, SHOPS, AND EVEN HOTEL ROOMS!

WAYMO

TRANSPORTATION OF TOMORROW

Three ... two ... one ... blast off! Going from here to there is going to be a lot bigger, better, and zoomier. Strap yourself in, and let's jet!

HYPERLOOP

Passenger capsules called transportation pods fill a tunnel that's lined with powerful magnets. The magnets lift the pods so that they float, reducing friction. Much of the air is removed from the tunnel so there's even less friction on the pods, letting them zoom at super "hyper" speeds.

SUPERSONIC JET

This incredibly fast, needle-shaped plane breaks the speed of sound and flies about 400 miles an hour (644 km/h) faster than today's airlines. You could fly around the world and be home in less time than it takes jet lag to set in!

REUSABLE ROCKETS

One reason rocket launches are so expensive today is that the rockets can be used only once. But reusable rockets survive the launch and can be used again. This reuse is better for the environment—and might mean that you could afford a ticket to Mars one day!

TERRAFUGIA TRANSITION

Push a button, and this two-seater transforms from car to plane. It uses regular gasoline and fits into a home garage, so there's no need to store it at an airport. Naturally, it comes equipped with airbags and a parachute.

Q'STRAINT

This robotic assistant can secure wheelchair riders on public transportation. Press a button and the robot fully secures a wheelchair in just 25 seconds.

SECURITY [EMMETT'S SECURITY SYSTEM & FANCHON'S HACKER TRACKER]

HOW IT WORKS AT THE ACADEMY

You're just getting out of survival training class when your tablet chimes. There's been a security breach in your dorm room! You hurry upstairs, wondering who could have tripped the series of motion detectors and infrared sensors you hid inside objects on your shelves. When you get to your room, you find the intruder: Hubbard, Taryn's dog! "How'd you get in here?" you ask. The dog in the plaid jacket can't say, but the crumbs around his mouth tell you what he was after. That's the last time you'll leave lunch out on your desk!

For Cruz, cybersecurity is a big deal. In Book 1: *The Nebula Secret,* Cruz's tablet is hacked by someone he could never suspect. In Book 2: *The Falcon's Feather,* Nebula breaks in and trashes his dorm room. This time, his roommate, Emmett, sets up some serious security. He rigs motion detectors, thermal sensors, infrared beams, and even cameras disguised as seashells. But then Nebula manages to hack into Cruz's diving helmet, almost drowning him! Fanchon builds a Hacker Tracker to find the culprit, but even with the best cybersecurity, Cruz learns, it's scarily difficult to stay ahead of determined hackers.

MAYBE FEASIBLE

NOT FEASIBLE

FEASIBLE

FEASIBILITY SCALE

[SECURITY SYSTEM] FEASIBILITY SCALE

HOW IT WORKS
IN REAL LIFE

"Spy cams" like Emmett's seashell cameras can be small enough to hide inside anything from a pair of glasses to a pen. (See more spy cameras on page 64.)

Motion sensors are real, too. Ultrasonic motion sensors work by projecting sound waves above the limit of what humans can hear. When the waves are interrupted by someone or something crossing through them, an alarm is triggered.

Thermal motion sensors are set off by body heat instead of sound. They detect sudden increases in infrared heat, which is the warmth all living things emit. (Learn more about infrared imaging on page 89.)

Photo motion sensors are activated by light. They project an invisible beam like a laser. Cross the beam, and an alarm will go off. *Gotcha!*

How Do Hacker Trackers Work?

Fanchon has an automatic "hacker tracker" to find intruders to her system. In real life, hackers are caught by "ethical hackers," people who work in teams to disable viruses or harmful software called malware. They look for clues, such as parts of a program's coding that have been translated into a foreign language.

One of the coolest cracked clues? A hacker called Guccifer used a smiley face in his coding that was different from the American style. Ethical hackers figured out it was an Eastern European–style smiley, and this discovery eventually led to his arrest!

[HACKER TRACKER]
FEASIBILITY SCALE

MAYBE FEASIBLE

FEASIBLE

FEASIBILITY SCALE

Banks, stores, and websites are vulnerable to hacking. The bigger the website, the more valuable it can be—packed with personal information that hackers can sell or use to access people's bank accounts or credit cards. Just think of what Nebula would do with Explorer Academy's student database!

Fortunately, there are things everyone can do to stay safe, starting with your passwords. When you go online and make an account for a website with a parent's permission, it's best to avoid short passwords you can remember easily. Generally, if you can easily remember a password, it's easy to hack. Birth dates, street names, and names of family, friends, pets, and even favorite characters are easy to hack. One way to build a strong password is to creatively substitute a sentence. For instance, a substitute for "Aunt Marisol loves studying anthropology" could be "AmlooovsstdygAnThRo54!"

Then, when a program asks if you want to use multi-factor identification, say yes. It means that your parent's phone or email will be sent a verification code that you'll need before you can enter a separate website or app. Getting that code will slow you down, but it'll *also* slow down hackers.

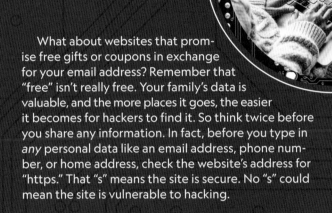

What about websites that promise free gifts or coupons in exchange for your email address? Remember that "free" isn't really free. Your family's data is valuable, and the more places it goes, the easier it becomes for hackers to find it. So think twice before you share any information. In fact, before you type in *any* personal data like an email address, phone number, or home address, check the website's address for "https." That "s" means the site is secure. No "s" could mean the site is vulnerable to hacking.

What NOT to Click!

The wrong click could open your digital door to hackers. Here's what to avoid.

> Ever hear of "clickbait"? Tempting quizzes like "Which Superhero Are You?" could be a secret way to collect your data. Some quiz creators can even grab access to your friends, hijack your account, or send you malware.

> Beware of random apps, which can come with an unwanted helping of malware. If the app doesn't have many positive reviews or it wasn't recommended by a trusted friend, skip it.

> If you get an email from a stranger (especially if it has an attachment), leave it alone and always tell an adult. It could be from a hacker sending a special delivery—malware.

THERMAL IMAGING

[LANI'S FLASHLIGHT]

HOW IT WORKS IN THE BOOK

In Book 3: *The Double Helix*, Cruz fearfully watches his tablet screen as Lani, who's back on Hawaii, takes a big risk. She's exploring an abandoned sugar mill that Cruz told her to avoid. Nebula could be waiting there! But according to a clue Cruz found, his missing dad could be there, too. Lani promised she'd stay away, but she didn't keep her word.

Lani quickly deploys her latest invention. It looks like a flashlight. She used her tech-savvy to give it a souped-up supercharge with an added ultrasensitive thermal imager. If anyone has touched anything within the last 24 hours, heat from their body, which has been absorbed by the environment—kind of the way a seat stays warm after you get up and walk away—will show up on the gadget's screen.

Lani's flashlight finds something! It's two pieces of silverware bound in the form of an X by something totally unexpected: Cruz's dad's necklace. Unfortunately, the flashlight doesn't double as an octopod. Because just then, someone else arrives and Cruz's tablet screen goes black!

[THERMAL IMAGING] FEASIBILITY SCALE

MAYBE FEASIBLE
NOT FEASIBLE
FEASIBLE
FEASIBILITY SCALE

HOW IT WORKS IN REAL LIFE

Thermal imaging is already possible, and there are even handheld thermal imaging cameras with built-in flashlights similar to Lani's. FLIR, the company that makes military thermal imagers, recently launched FLIR ONE, a mini thermal imaging camera that attaches to your cellphone. The tech works by detecting infrared light, which are light waves that all living things radiate but human eyes can't see. Thermal imaging cameras can detect infrared waves through darkness, smoke, and even blankets. This is different from tech called night vision, which you might have heard of. Night vision amplifies surrounding light, but it doesn't work in complete darkness.

In contrast, thermal imaging cameras scan invisible-to-us infrared light, then generate what's called a thermogram—a temperature pattern—and use that to construct an image. On your device's screen, you'll see either black (in the case of black-and-white imagers) or orange and yellow wherever there are infrared waves.

A THERMAL IMAGING CAMERA CATCHES MOVEMENT AND INFRARED LIGHT.

Whichever tech you choose, seeing in the dark can be handy. Explorers can spot bears inside their dens without disturbing the animals. Researchers can find feverish people in a crowd and pinpoint an epidemic. You could even locate your lost pet in the dark. Now here's a piece of tech Fido would approve of!

WHOLE BRAIN EMULATION
[TIME CAPSULE]

HOW IT WORKS AT THE ACADEMY

You cup a purple capsule in your hand, then squeeze it in your fist. It jiggles a little, signaling that it's ready. You close your eyes and think of the incredible time you had today with your teammates, solving riddles from Taryn and conquering a crazy obstacle course. You don't want to forget a single detail. And now you won't, because the time capsule just recorded your memory so you can replay it anytime!

In Book 3: *The Falcon's Feather*, Fanchon is about to give up on her UCC helmet because it was hacked, but Cruz has an idea to change her mind. If you could show Fanchon a memory that would keep her working on her inventions, what would it be?

[TIME CAPSULE] FEASIBILITY SCALE

HOW IT WORKS IN REAL LIFE

No computer can detect and upload memories straight from your brain ... *yet.* But scientists are working on it. Whole brain emulation (WBE) is one possibility under study. WBE is the idea that an exact copy of your brain could be made, creating an identical software version of it—basically creating a backup drive of everything you've ever thought, felt, and experienced.

A STUDENT TRIES ON AN ELECTROENCEPHALOGRAM (EEG), WHICH RECORDS ELECTRICAL ACTIVITY OF THE BRAIN.

As wild as that may sound, scientists have already managed to transfer memories between snails. In a study, one group of snails was trained to respond to an impulse. Each time they felt the impulse, their tails curled. Then genetic information from the trained snails' nerve tissue was injected into a second group of untrained snails. And those snails curled their tails just like the trained snails had! That suggests that memories, or at least snails' memories, are stored inside nerve cells.

Identifying memories' location in the human body would be a big deal, but many scientists still disagree about where we store our memories. Once they find out for certain, memories could become a powerful healing tool. Doctors might be able to reprogram painful memories and reduce post-traumatic stress disorder, or make positive memories easier to access, kind of like a real-life time capsule.

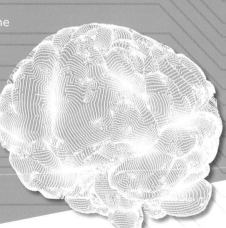

FUTURE BRAINS

NEW NOGGIN

What would happen if instead of storing or replacing single memories, you could swap out your old brain for a computerized version? Talk about changing your mind!

A BRAIN SCAN

Scientists are working on it. The first step: implantable memory chips that could give you perfect recall, similar to the Time Capsule. That would be handy before a test—no more studying!

But what about replacing your entire brain?

Some neurologists compare this to any other prosthesis. If your hip wears out, you can replace it. So why not your brain? After all, a replacement hip could make you feel better, but a replacement brain could make you last long after your original body is gone. In fact, a copy of your brain could be uploaded to a new body, making you basically immortal. Some scientists argue that connecting neurons to a new body would be tricky if not impossible. But if it did work, you could customize your new form. How about a mermaid tail or a unicorn horn? You could customize your brain, too. Just upload a library of foreign languages or a suite of dance moves for instant new abilities.

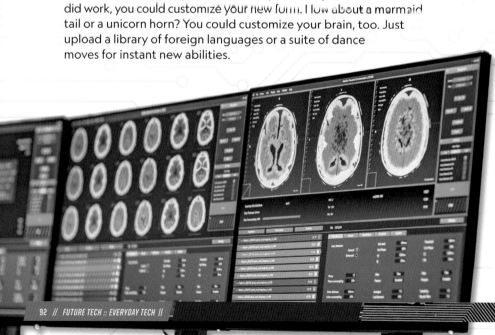

FREE THINKING

What if your new brain could go body-free and be hosted by a computer, so anyone you approve could access it? Future explorers could collaborate with you! Having infinite time to solve the world's problems might mean finally overcoming Earth's toughest challenges.

So how close are we to copying brains? We're pretty far. Scientists still don't know where thinking, personality, and feelings are located in our brains, so making backups of those isn't possible *yet*. But according to some futurists (people who study world trends and predict future developments), it's only a matter of time.

WHAT WOULD YOU DO WITH
DOWNLOADED MEMORIES?

If you could flip through memories like photos, what could you do with them?

- [ ] Delete ones you don't like
- [ ] Prove you were right about something in the past
- [ ] Trade with friends
- [ ] Change them to make them better
- [ ] Buy "designer" memories, such as hanging out with a celebrity or going on safari
- [ ] Donate them to people who have lost theirs
- [ ] Give happy memories to your family and friends as a gift

TRANSFORMATIONAL TECH

Sometimes, an invention comes along that changes how people see and experience the world. Before Wi-Fi, it was hard to imagine a phone that wasn't connected to the wall, or a way to contact international friends besides air mail (which took weeks). Now, can you picture being unreachable on vacation ... or even in the car?

Transformational tech completely reimagines how things can work. For instance, instead of playing video games on a screen, you could step into the CAVE and use augmented reality to play with holograms that appear in midair. And you probably don't think objects can suddenly transform before your eyes, but that's exactly what programmable materials—like Cruz's mom's journal—can do. Even farms might be disrupted by supertechie greenhouses like the one aboard *Orion!*

Get ready to see a lot of things differently, thanks to transformational tech.

A VIRTUAL-REALITY DRIVING GAME

VIRTUAL, AUGMENTED, AND MIXED REALITY
[CAVE]

HOW IT WORKS AT THE ACADEMY

You step through a door marked CAVE, or Computer Animated Virtual Experience. Minutes earlier, this room was a huge, empty space. But now, it's a vast forest beneath an open sky! A butterfly lands on your hand, tickling your skin. Wind blows softly, and the sun warms your face. Yet none of it is real. It's a simulation using climate control, 3D printing (for robots like the butterfly), and holograms. When you touch a hologram, it reacts with heat from your body so you can feel it!

Cruz is starting orientation in Book 1: *The Nebula Secret* when he's taken to the CAVE. He hears a low grunt ... soft thunder ... then he feels a rumble. A cloud of dust explodes around him. It's a wildebeest stampede! Most of Cruz's team hits the floor or runs. It turns out there's nothing to be afraid of. The dust has been piped in through vents, the sounds came from speakers, and the wildebeests are holograms. Still, the CAVE isn't all virtual. On one mission, Cruz gets a taste of "mixed reality" when moving sets create a high waterfall that he tries to leap over. He actually falls and lands on a crash mat!

The CAVE isn't the only way Cruz and his team experience mixed reality. They also have helmets that make objects suddenly appear as they navigate a real obstacle course. The helmets are like CAVEs that can go anywhere!

HOW IT WORKS IN REAL LIFE

Several companies have already produced goggles that make 3D robots, animals, or whole environments appear before your eyes. You might see a cheetah cub sitting in your desk chair or a pterodactyl flying around your ceiling fan. One company, called Magic Leap, has made working virtual computer screens that hover in space, a virtual TV that plays shows on four different sides, and even virtual people who can follow your gaze and talk to you.

Each company's goggles or glasses work a little differently, but they all use lenses to create 3D images. These lenses combine natural light from the room with a digitally produced image and send both to your eyes at the same time, tricking you into seeing 3D holograms. To make the holograms appear right where a program wants them to be (like a goblin in your closet), a camera in the glasses records the real world. It recognizes landmarks like corners and doors. Then it creates "markers" that pinpoint spots in your environment to display the computer images.

Unlike the experience at Explorer Academy, you can't feel the images that virtual reality produces. But you can go to virtual-reality amusement parks, which have sets that include sound, wind, and other sensory effects.

MAYBE FEASIBLE

FEASIBLE

NOT FEASIBLE

FEASIBILITY SCALE

[CAVE] FEASIBILITY SCALE

AUGMENTED AND MIXED REALITY

The CAVE isn't the only way you could experience virtual reality in the near future. At virtual-reality games theaters, you can put on a headset, grab a simulated tool for combat, and step into an arena to do battle with other players! If playful fighting isn't your thing, you can try a virtual-reality theatrical performance. At the University of Iowa, students and faculty collaborated to create a play in which audience members wear VR headsets while interacting with live players.

AN AUDIENCE MEMBER USES A VR HEADSET AT A NATIONAL GEOGRAPHIC LIVE EVENT.

Are you more an observer? You can sit back in your seat and let virtual reality come to you. Events at National Geographic Headquarters use VR videos to take viewers to ancient lands and real places around the world, no hiking necessary.

Virtual reality works in practical ways, too. Google is developing a new navigation feature that will make sure you don't miss a tricky turn. While you're walking, just hold up your phone to the real world, and the app will display it with arrows on top, pointing exactly where to go. The effect is called augmented reality because it adds to (augments) what you see. It's not quite GPS sunglasses, but it's close!

A PLAY AT THE UNIVERSITY OF IOWA USING VR HEADSETS

WHAT'S NEXT FOR AUGMENTED AND MIXED REALITY?

Virtual reality is changing so fast, there's a new abbreviation for it: XR, where the X stands for all types of digitally altered reality— augmented, mixed, and some that haven't been invented yet. And in the future, there will be lots of XR things you can do.

How about checking out a party in Singapore today and another in San Diego tomorrow? Getting there would be expensive if not impossible. But at XR parties, you can be there in an instant. Just put on your headset! Even better, people of all physical abilities can mix and mingle without any obstacles to travel.

Want to rearrange your room, but not lug around furniture? You could put on an XR headset and see how everything would look in different spots. Or you could virtually clean your room without actually doing it—just make sure your parents wear their headsets before they walk in!

XR has serious uses, too. It can help to guide a surgeon by projecting a map of the inside of the body on a patient's skin. That same surgeon could add remote technology, and operate on someone in another country.

UNEXPECTED PLACES
YOU'LL FIND VR

You can probably think of a lot of uses for virtual reality ...
but we bet you wouldn't guess these.

FRUIT FLY GAMING

You know those tiny bugs, scientifically known as *Drosophila melanogaster*, that hang around fruit bowls? Well, they like virtual reality, too. A scientific study introduced fruit flies to virtual-reality video games. As silly as that sounds, consider this. It appears that the bitty bugs can play them! The simple game involves moving a dark bar by flying around. Scientists who measured the insects' brain activity found that the fruit flies were apparently figuring out their next moves. Some were better players than others. The result: Fruit flies may be self-aware, which means there's a lot more to their consciousness than humans ever knew. And, oh yeah, they might beat you at Minecraft.

BUGGING OUT

Lots of people are afraid of creepy crawlies. Now, they can get over their fears by meeting them head-on ... virtually. Virtual bugs are being used to help people overcome their fear of the real ones. Interacting with the insects in a safe way seems to reduce phobias. Plus you don't have to worry about getting bitten.

TAKING COCKROACHES ON A FIELD TRIP

Studying roaches' brain activity pretty much has to be done in a lab; setting them free risks losing them (and really freaking out your lab partner). But scientists have found a way to study them on "forest floors" using virtual reality. Roaches can now wander through a virtual forest while researchers track their reactions to the *almost*-real environment.

SURVIVING BLACK FRIDAY

The holiday rush is one of the biggest challenges for new department store employees. Enter: virtual reality Black Friday! Walmart is training workers to deal with holiday madness and in-aisle messes through a virtual simulator. While one employee interacts with VR, a big screen displays what he or she is seeing, so that employees without headsets can watch and learn, too.

LEARNING TO WALK

Paraplegics in a study at Duke University were given VR headsets that created a scene in which the volunteers were soccer players moving across a field. All of the eight volunteers regained some control of their legs—some of them significantly! Researchers found that the longer volunteers practiced with the headsets, the better the chances they'd regain control of their bodies. In the future, more volunteers might be able to participate through the internet.

4.0 TRANSFORMATIONAL TECH

4D PRINTING [PETRA'S JOURNAL]

HOW IT WORKS AT THE ACADEMY

Cruz is moments away from being obliterated by a killer in Book 1: *The Nebula Secret* when a piece of paper saves him. Just before the bad guy fires a laser at Cruz, what seemed to be a bookmark starts moving by itself, then folds into a complex origami sculpture. The killer is so startled, he lowers his weapon!

An orange light appears on one of the paper sculpture's points and scans the attacker. Not finding what it's after, it scans Cruz instead. A 3D hologram of Cruz's mom appears and starts speaking to him. She reveals that this self-folding paper is her secret journal, and it contains clues that will lead him to the lifesaving serum she invented. Every time he finds a cipher piece, the journal will unlock another clue. But each discovery comes with extreme danger, and his mom urges Cruz to carefully consider if he wants to take on the job. Cruz doesn't hesitate. The serum was his mom's life work. Now, finding it is his most important mission!

MAYBE FEASIBLE

NOT FEASIBLE

FEASIBLE

FEASIBILITY SCALE

[PETRA'S JOURNAL] FEASIBILITY SCALE

HOW IT WORKS IN REAL LIFE

National Geographic Explorer Skylar Tibbits and other scientists are engineering materials that can fold themselves. As founder and co-director of the Self-Assembly Lab at Massachusetts Institute of Technology, Tibbits is the inventor of "4D" printing. The fourth "D," or dimension, stands for time, because that's what it takes for the materials to transform.

Temperature, pressure, water, electricity, or light can all trigger the change to start. One of Tibbits' first 4D creations was a water-absorbent material that can be programmed to take on any geometric shape when it's wet. This transformation is fun to watch and can potentially save a great deal of time in manufacturing.

A 4D-PRINTED SINGLE STRAND TRANSFORMED INTO A 3-DIMENSIONAL CUBE

Tibbits and his team have gone on to create shoes that are printed as flat sheets and assemble themselves. "We used a stretch textile," says Tibbits. "The stretch is embedded energy in the system like a jack-in-the-box effect." It makes the shoe jump into shape!

Tibbits points out that some of his creations are more accurately called "programmable materials" because they aren't 3D printed, but they still transform. "The printing was because we hadn't figured out how we could do it in any other way," Tibbits says. Now, he's experimenting with laminations and bonding. This tech could be used someday to create furniture that builds itself, or even replacement body parts like heart valves that automatically adjust inside the body. Tibbits' team is also looking into ways to make yarn and textiles transform. Maybe real-life Explorer Academy uniforms will be possible in the not too distant future!

MORE DEVELOPMENTS IN 4D
AND PROGRAMMABLE MATERIALS

A journal that changes forms is amazing, but even more incredible: a 4D product that changes lives. Here are some areas in which 4D and programmable materials are unfolding onto the scene.

AIRWAY OPENERS

Doctors at the University of Michigan's C.S. Mott Children's Hospital have developed a 4D-printed airway splint to help babies with severe breathing problems. The tiny splints keep infants' windpipes open. Their 4D powers kick in when the splints expand as the babies grow! They keep expanding until the children are strong enough to breathe on their own.

COOL IDEA

If you've ever worked up a sweat just sitting inside a stuffy plane, you might appreciate Airbus's programmable carbon fiber. This invention, currently in development, will one day help cool the plane's engine by automatically adjusting, controlling airflow to the engine. That adjustment will also regulate cabin pressure, making the air in the plane more comfortable to breathe.

WIDER WATER

When flooding sends a huge amount of water through sewer pipes, it can stress pipes enough to burst them. Programmable pipes could fix that problem by contracting or expanding with high or low water flow. Pipes could also be programmed to bend but not break during an earthquake!

DO-IT-THEMSELVES

Why do heavy lifting when the materials can do it for you? Engineers are working on materials that will build themselves into houses. On a smaller scale, ready-to-assemble furniture that comes in a box will be able to assemble itself! And if you still need help, there are always robots. Futurists predict that robots will one day be able to design, assemble, and 4D-print themselves.

A HEAVY-LIFTING MACHINE IN A FACTORY

BETTER BRACES

No one wants repeat visits to the orthodontist to tighten braces on their teeth. That's why a French company is working on a way to scan your mouth and then 3D-print orthodontics that can automatically adjust when your teeth need it!

IT'S ALIVE!

You might someday live in a house whose walls are alive, thanks to engineered living materials (ELM). These building materials would be made using microorganisms such as cells, bacteria, or even DNA. As the living components grow, they might release substances that protect or strengthen structures, or they could self-generate whole buildings!

HOLOGRAMS [HOLO-VIDEO]

HOW IT WORKS AT THE ACADEMY

Y ou cup a silvery metal dome in the palm of your hand. When it touches your skin, it switches on. Your Explorer Academy teammates appear in a 3D hologram, hovering above the dome! You watch them cheer as they win Monsieur Legrand's crazy obstacle course. Who needs video when you've got holo-video? By replaying the action, you can work on perfecting your moves for next time. The images are so detailed, it's almost better than experiencing it in person!

When Cruz misses his mom, he takes a moment to watch his holo-video. It shows his mom and Cruz when he was a toddler. The holo-video is precious to him, but he doesn't realize exactly *how* precious it is until he's trying to solve his mom's first clue to finding a cipher piece. In Book 1: *The Nebula Secret,* Lani suggests the holo-video may have something to do with solving the clue. And sure enough, the silvery dome is hiding a secret of its own!

MAYBE FEASIBLE

NOT FEASIBLE

FEASIBLE

FEASIBILITY SCALE

[HOLO-VIDEO] FEASIBILITY SCALE

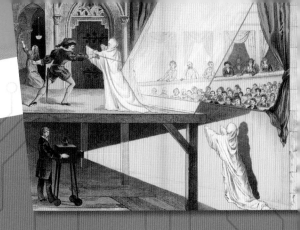

HOW IT WORKS
IN REAL LIFE

Dedicated holo-video players don't exist yet. But if someone tells you their phone works as a holographic video player, they're *kind* of right. They could show you a "holographic video" through a 3D hologram pyramid that attaches to their screen. Images appear to hang in midair! Still, those aren't technically holograms.

The effect is actually an *illusion* of holograms based on a trick called "Pepper's Ghost." A British scientist, John H. Pepper, perfected the technique of placing a piece of glass at an angle that covers a dark corner of a brightly lit stage. An actor dressed as a ghost hides in the dark corner. When the lights on the stage are dimmed and the lights in the dark corner are turned up, the hidden actor appears as a ghostly reflection. Now that's seriously spooky!

Today, "Pepper's Ghosts" can look like real living people thanks to high-quality video projections. The effect has been used at concerts to make performers who are no longer alive seem to appear onstage.

MAKE YOUR OWN HOLO-VIDEO VIEWER

This pyramid viewer on a phone creates a mini version of Pepper's Ghost.

1. With adult supervision, carefully cut out four identical triangles with flat bottoms out of pieces of firm, clear plastic.
2. Connect the pieces using tape to make a pyramid.
3. Put the pyramid on the center of a cell phone screen with the wide base facing up.
4. Turn down the lights.
5. Play a hologram video and the images will "float" in the pyramid!

HOLOGRAMS OF THE FUTURE

Holo-video players like Cruz's may not exist yet, but holograms are being used now to do things that might impress you even more.

URBAN PHOTONIC SANDTABLE DISPLAY (UPSD)

Developed for military use, this holographic map can make entire cities pop up before your eyes—no AR goggles or glasses required! Military engineers are also working on lifelike hologram projections that could show up on a battlefield and scare enemy troops into retreating, kind of like the zombies Cruz sees at the CAVE Halloween party. *Boo!*

DEEPFRAME

Look through this window and see the real world *plus* added 3D holograms or hovering text (similar to what the Explorers see through their sunglasses when they look at historical sites). This tech could be used to holographically project you into a room across the world, or maybe to show you a living dinosaur when you look at its bones!

THE LOOKING GLASS IS A HOLOGRAPHIC DISPLAY THAT ALLOWS PEOPLE TO VIEW AND INTERACT WITH 3D HOLOGRAMS.

THE LOOKING GLASS

Just as your brain forms a single image out of two unique views from your eyes, the Looking Glass joins multiple views of an object or scene to make 3D holograms. Plug it into a PC and watch worlds come to holographic life, and move from side to side to see around or even behind holograms—just like in the movies!

HOLOGRAPHIC FILM

Holograms make pretty good journals, too (which might be why Cruz's mom chose one for *her* journal). Holographic film can handle huge amounts of info because it stores data in three dimensions! Plus if you break a hologram that contains information, you can reconstruct the whole thing from a fragment.

FUTURE SHIPS [ORION]

HOW IT WORKS AT THE ACADEMY

You stand before the 364-foot (111-m) ship and look up. The CAVE simulation of *Orion* was amazing, but it was nothing compared to the real thing! You eagerly dash to your cabin, which has an attached balcony, and drop your bags. You know from the CAVE simulation that there's much more to see. You hurry upstairs to see the classrooms and labs. On an upper deck, you find a two-story library with a giant glass map covering the ceiling. The top deck even has a helipad. You hope you'll get to take a flight!

You jog down from deck to deck and find a mini CAVE. Wait what's this unmarked door that your OS band won't open? Could it be a secret lab, maybe even the Synthesis? You'll have to do some exploring to find out!

Cruz and his team sail on *Orion* for missions to every continent and take classes on board. With all its tech, the ship seems safe. But is it? Cruz learns not everyone on *Orion* is friendly. And being in the middle of the ocean with Nebula along for the ride means Cruz will need all the ship's resources—including whatever's behind that mysterious locked door—to stay alive.

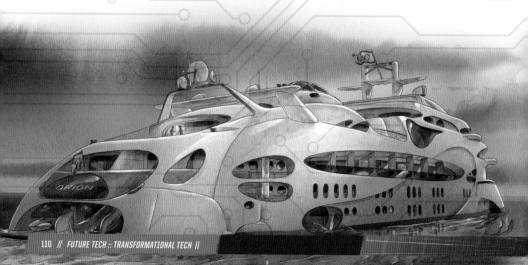

QUEEN MARY 2 PLANETARIUM

REAL-LIFE INSPIRATION

There is a boat called *Orion* in National Geographic's fleet, but another vessel in the fleet is even more similar to Explorer Academy's *Orion:* the *National Geographic Explorer*. This ship travels from pole to pole each year, spending winters in Antarctica and summers in the Arctic. It's equipped with video to observe underwater life such as orcas, seals, and polar bears. It carries a fleet of motorized rafts specially designed to bring explorers within selfie distance of animals and icebergs. Like Explorer Academy's *Orion*, the ship also carries an undersea specialist, a photography instructor, a video chronicler, a doctor, and a wellness specialist.

Explorer isn't the only tricked-out vessel on the open ocean. Royal Caribbean's *Quantum of the Seas* features something called Virtual Balconies, which are digital screens that display real-time images of what's outside. The ship also has a skydiving simulator!

Disney Fantasy, a cruise ship, uses tech for entertainment, too. Onboard "Enchanted Art" looks like a painting, but when you get close, the pictures move! *Carnival Breeze* has a 5D theater that shows 3D movies you can feel. Seats move, water sprays, and something might even tickle your feet.

Tech on Cunard's *Queen Mary 2* is more practical. The ship has an 11-bed hospital with an x-ray machine and lab, and a reverse osmosis machine to make seawater drinkable. But it's not all serious. There's also a planetarium!

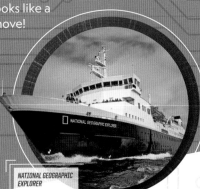

NATIONAL GEOGRAPHIC EXPLORER

MORE SUPER SHIPS

Seafaring technology is making break-throughs every day. For an eco-friendly update, *Orion*'s designers might want to check out the *NYK Super Eco Ship 2050*, a concept ship (meaning it's been brainstormed but not yet built). It promises to use 67 percent less fossil fuel than similar ships made in 2014. The ship will conserve fossil fuels, a limited natural resource, by using hydrogen to power the boat's onboard fuel cells and solar panels.

Aquarius Eco Ship, a cargo ship from Japan, is another concept ship that aims to reduce fossil fuels, but it has a different approach and a different look. How about hard-sided sails that stand up like giant playing cards? The rigid sails may be mounted with solar panels and wind-powered devices.

Cargo ships are being updated, too. The *E/S Orcelle* is being designed to transport 10,000 cars while running on wind, solar, and wave energy. Some of that energy will be converted into hydrogen to power fuel cells that run the ship.

And there's a vessel without a captain. Rolls-Royce's autonomous ship plans to use companion drones as scouts. A hologram of the ship's systems will let operators on land watch for any trouble and be ready to fix it!

SEAWORTHY INVENTIONS

These shipshape inventions make boats that are more efficient *and* gentler on the environment.

ROTOR BOATS

Viking Grace, the first liquefied natural gas (LNG)-powered cruise ship, has a "rotor sail" to capture power from wind. The sail looks more like a giant column with a turbine inside. It could reduce the ship's CO_2 emissions by 1,000 tons (907 t) per year!

BUBBLE BLAST

"Air lubrication" is a technique that pumps a layer of bubbles below a flat-bottomed ship. These bubbles reduce friction and the amount of energy the ship needs to move. For extra-smooth sailing, painting a ship with low-friction coating can lower a boat's energy needs.

RIGHT TURN

Instead of using one propeller, some ships are using two. When they're placed one behind the other and spin in opposite directions, the energy from the first propeller helps to power the second one. This system makes the ship up to 15 percent more efficient!

FUTURISTIC FARMING
[THE GREENHOUSE]

HOW IT WORKS AT THE ACADEMY

Broccoli and lettuce heads brush your elbows. Twirling vines of sugar snap peas curl up walls. Bright red tomatoes, orange peppers, and juicy strawberries hang everywhere you look. *Orion's* onboard greenhouse could rival any farm on land. You gaze up at a bubbled glass ceiling, then at the solar-powered laser lights that keep the greenhouse plants growing at all hours. You wonder what Chef Kristos will harvest for tonight's dinner. Breathing deeply, you smell oregano and sage, and your stomach rumbles. Here's hoping for spaghetti marinara!

Tasty as that food sounds, Cruz and his teammates hope the greenhouse can harvest something totally different in Book 3: *The Double Helix*. They need to fix Cruz's mom's journal, and if their theories are right, the greenhouse has exactly what they need. Cruz winds up sleeping all night on the greenhouse's steamy floor, waiting to see if his plan works. It's a risk—he could get caught staying out past curfew. But compared to the danger of Nebula finding him, camping among the plants and leaves feels refreshingly safe!

[THE GREENHOUSE] FEASIBILITY SCALE

HOW IT WORKS IN REAL LIFE

With more than 7.5 billion people living on Earth, the future of our food supply is a major area of focus. So greenhouses, which can yield 10 to 12 times more produce than field crops, are a hot spot for new technology.

Altius Farms in Colorado, U.S.A., boasts one of the most cutting-edge greenhouses around. Its plants grow on vertical towers. These space-savers turn out 10 times as much as conventional farming ... with a tenth of the water!

At Advanced Crop Lab in Durham, North Carolina, U.S.A., dozens of rooms can be programmed with their own microclimates. Wide-spectrum lights mimic sunshine, like on *Orion,* while the roof has two layers separated by an inch of argon gas, which helps keep an even temperature. The plants have a high-tech feeding system, too: In "fertigation," computer-controlled tubes send water and nutrients to each pot!

MAKE A MINI GREENHOUSE!

You'll need: Two clear drinking cups, soil, seeds (carrot, parsley, or basil work well). It's best to use recycled or used clear cups.

1. Place soil and plant seeds in a cup, filling it about 1/3 of the way, following package instructions.
2. Moisten the soil.
3. Make three small holes in the second cup. Then tape the second cup on top of the first cup to create a greenhouse.
4. When the plant outgrows the greenhouse, it's time to repot!

PLANTS IN SPACE

Someday, humans may be able to tour other planets, or even live in outer space. To do that for long stretches of time, we'll need food. Freeze-dried meals don't last forever. That's why NASA has been working on farming in space.

Outer space's big swings in light, temperature, and gravity are huge stressors for Earth plants. Spaceflight also causes problems in plants, including thin cell walls, shorter roots, and poor growth. Biologists have figured out how to change some plants' genetics so they can overcome these issues.

To thrive in space, plants still need special growing conditions. On the International Space Station, which is a laboratory in orbit, there are colored LEDs and "plant pillows" that contain seeds, special fertilizer, and clay. Watering is tricky because water won't flow without Earth's gravity, so automated systems take care of that. And fans move the air because vital carbon dioxide and oxygen will be stuck in place otherwise.

MIZUNA LETTUCE GROWING ON INTERNATIONAL SPACE STATION

Researchers from China recently sent a variety of seeds to the moon. The seeds were contained in a "biosphere"—a container that also held yeast and fruit fly eggs. Researchers were excited when cotton seeds sprouted ... but the sprouts died a week later from the moon's icy cold nights. Nothing else in that biosphere survived.

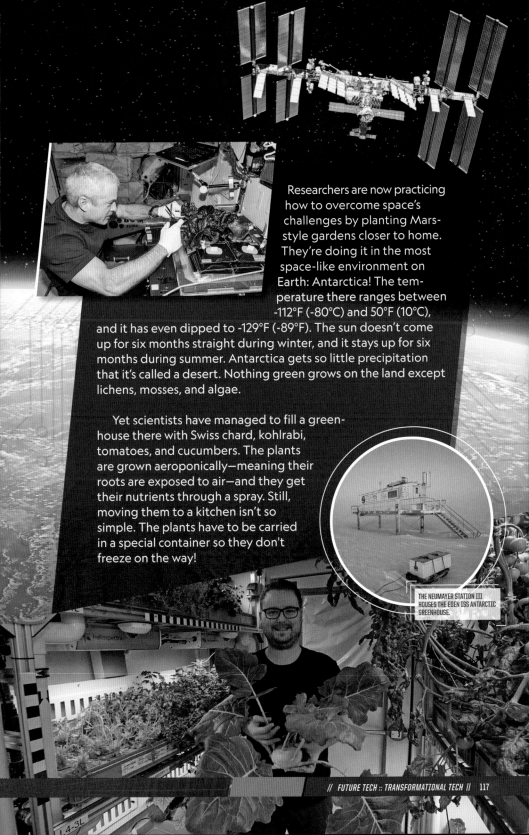

Researchers are now practicing how to overcome space's challenges by planting Mars-style gardens closer to home. They're doing it in the most space-like environment on Earth: Antarctica! The temperature there ranges between -112°F (-80°C) and 50°F (10°C), and it has even dipped to -129°F (-89°F). The sun doesn't come up for six months straight during winter, and it stays up for six months during summer. Antarctica gets so little precipitation that it's called a desert. Nothing green grows on the land except lichens, mosses, and algae.

Yet scientists have managed to fill a greenhouse there with Swiss chard, kohlrabi, tomatoes, and cucumbers. The plants are grown aeroponically—meaning their roots are exposed to air—and they get their nutrients through a spray. Still, moving them to a kitchen isn't so simple. The plants have to be carried in a special container so they don't freeze on the way!

THE NEUMAYER STATION III HOUSES THE EDEN ISS ANTARCTIC GREENHOUSE.

URBAN PLANNING
[EXPLORER ACADEMY CAMPUS]

HOW IT WORKS AT THE ACADEMY

Some of Explorer Academy's most fun features are part of the campus itself. Many of them are inspired by real campuses and cities throughout the world.

CONFIDENTIAL CLASSIFIED LAB: **THE SYNTHESIS**

To get inside Explorer Academy's highest-security lab, you'll need to pass iris biometric identification. A scanner identifies you by unique patterns in the colored parts of your eyes! And you're in luck, this tech is already available in cell phones today.

INSIDE THE SYNTHESIS: **BULLETPROOF GLASS**

Bulletproof glass is a sandwich of many layers of glass and plastic. When a bullet hits bulletproof glass, these layers help absorb the bullet's energy and slow it down. Still, no glass is completely bulletproof. An impact with enough force will shatter it (don't tell Nebula!).

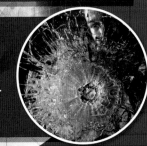

THE CLASSROOMS

The front wall of each class features nine thin computer screens. In schools across America, you're likely to see "interactive whiteboards," which are images projected from a computer. Instead of writing on a blackboard, your teacher types, or clicks a mouse.

THE NORTH STAR PYRAMID

The six-foot (1.8-m)-tall crystal pyramid inscribed with names of North Star winners is a close cousin to architect I. M. Pei's famous glass-and-metal pyramid in front of the Louvre Museum in Paris.

DORM ROOMS

Cruz's room has a real-time view of Everest on one wall, streaming live from one of the base camps. Wall-size video monitors exist today and so does the world's highest web-cam, which points at the summit of Mount Everest!

THE LIBRARY

The ceiling of this five-leveled room is painted with stars in the same formation as the night the Society, and the real National Geographic Society, was founded, January 27, 1888. National Geographic headquarters has a ceiling like this.

FUTURE SCHOOLS

You don't have to get into Explorer Academy to have a *tech-tastic* class. Technology is already changing schools all over the world. You'll find 3D printers, digital cameras, and coding labs popping up everywhere. In fact, instead of giving homework, some schools are asking students to spend more time in the maker labs, coming up with inventions. It's easy to imagine Fanchon giving that assignment.

Other new schools don't have walls at all. At THINK Global School, a steep tuition lets students live in a different country each semester. It might be the closest thing to becoming an Explorer!

Check out these international ideas—they might soon be coming to a classroom near you.

UK: VIRTUAL-REALITY CLASSROOM

On a VR field trip, kids visit museums and historical places without leaving homeroom.

SEVENOAKS SCHOOL

SHIDHULAI SWANIRVAR SANGSTHA SCHOOL

BANGLADESH: SOLAR-POWERED FLOATING SCHOOLS

During monsoon season, students board these schools and use a laptop to access textbooks and the library.

BALI: WALLS, TABLES, FLOORS, AND CHAIRS MADE OF SUSTAINABLE BAMBOO

Using this natural material teaches students about sustainability.

EMPOWER PLAYGROUNDS, INC.

GHANA: A MERRY-GO-ROUND CHARGER

When kids play on this merry-go-round, it charges a battery. Later, they can use the light they've produced to read at night.

CANADA: NO DESKS OR PAPER

Kids hang out on bouncy balls or on the floor, and use tablets instead of notebooks.

SINGAPORE: ROBOT ASSISTANT TEACHERS

How about an assistant teacher who isn't human? A robot can answer pretty much all your questions and check your work.

FUTURE CITIES

Since the Explorer Academy series takes place in the near future, the cities Cruz and his teammates visit are filled with exciting technology. We can imagine what they might be like because of changes already underway around the world—changes that are coming soon to cities near you.

Sustainable City in Dubai is an eco-conscious housing development that has many of the features you'll see in our city of the future, below. The result: a city that's gentle on the environment *and* almost runs by itself.

NARROWER STREETS
Self-driving cars don't need wide roads because they navigate more precisely than humans can.

MORE GREEN SPACES
Narrower roads and no street parking leave more space for plants and pedestrians.

CENTRAL PARKING AREA
Cars will park in one area because they can be called via app when they're needed.

DRONES
Flying or wheeled drones will come to your door to deliver groceries or packages.

INTELLIGENT TRANSPORT
No need to drive. Your car or bus will do it for you.

NORTH-FACING HOMES
Houses built to face north will get more shade and save energy.

A LAYOUT FOR APARTMENT HOMES IN SUSTAINABLE CITY IN DUBAI

SOLAR PANELS AND WIND TURBINES
These will generate energy that's friendly to the environment.

GRAY WATER FOUNTAINS
Untreated water from showers and sinks, called gray water, can be reused in decorative fountains that also irrigate plants.

BIODOME FARMS
These dome-shaped greenhouses can pop up all over cities, and grow the food needed to support the people there.

3D-PRINTED HOUSES
Some may even be 4D printed, meaning they'll build themselves!

UV-REFLECTIVE PAINT ON BUILDINGS
This paint reduces the amount of heat a building absorbs.

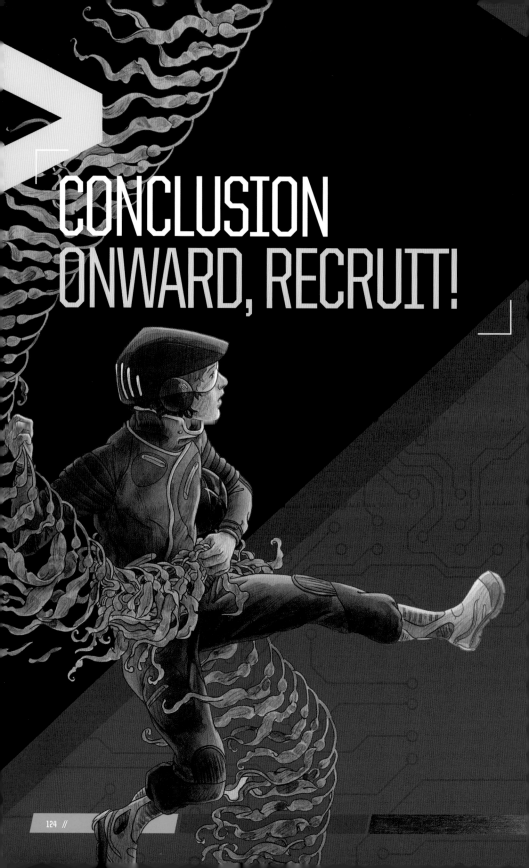

CONCLUSION
ONWARD, RECRUIT!

Congratulations on completing your Explorer Academy technology walk-through, new recruit! You've tested the best the Academy has to offer. We hope you feel inspired to take your knowledge and explorer skills into your world.

After all, the tech doesn't stop at the end of this book. As you now know, Explorer Academy's mind-bending gadgets and gizmos are quickly becoming reality. Every day, real-life scientists and National Geographic explorers around the world are designing inventions that will respond to our planet's changing needs. New tech is plunging into the deepest oceans, creeping through the longest caves, discovering the most remote jungles, and climbing the highest mountaintops. The goal is to save species, preserve geological landmarks, and even solve world problems for future generations.

But today's inventors can't do it alone.

That's where you come in, explorer. Chances are good that the next game-changing idea will be something no one has even thought of yet. Could you be the one to come up with it? Take a tip from Cruz and his teammates and start imagining!

 **Your wildest, craziest ideas might be the very ones to change the future.**

PHOTO CREDITS

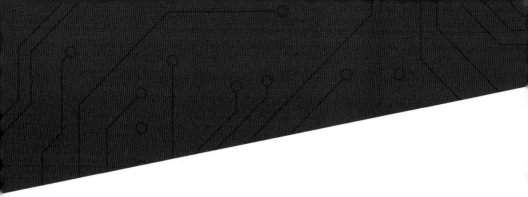

To you, for being brave enough to explore new ideas. You are the future! —Jamie Kiffel-Alcheh

Since 1888, the National Geographic Society has funded more than 12,000 research, exploration, and preservation projects around the world. The Society receives funds from National Geographic Partners, LLC, funded in part by your purchase. A portion of the proceeds from this book supports this vital work. To learn more, visit natgeo.com/info.

For more information, visit: nationalgeographic.com, call 1-877-873-6846, or write to the following address:

National Geographic Partners
1145 17th Street N.W.
Washington, DC 20036-4688 U.S.A.

Visit us online at nationalgeographic.com/books

For librarians and teachers: nationalgeographic.com/books/librarians-and-educators

More for kids from National Geographic: natgeokids.com

National Geographic Kids magazine inspires children to explore their world with fun yet educational articles on animals, science, nature, and more. Using fresh storytelling and amazing photography, *Nat Geo Kids* shows kids ages 6 to 14 the fascinating truth about the world—and why they should care. **kids.nationalgeographic.com/subscribe**

For rights or permissions inquiries, please contact National Geographic Books Subsidiary Rights: bookrights@natgeo.com

Designed by Rachael Hamm Plett, Moduza Design
Cover design by Eva Absher-Schantz

Trade Paperback ISBN: 978-1-4263-3914-1
Reinforced library binding ISBN: 978-1-4263-3915-8

The publisher would like to acknowledge the following people for making this book possible: Jamie Kiffel-Alcheh, author; Avery Naughton, project editor; Lori Epstein, director of photography; Eva Absher-Schantz, vice president of visual identity; Julie Beer, fact-checker; Vivian Suchman, managing editor; Joan Gossett, production editorial manager; and Anne LeongSon and Gus Tello, design production assistants.

Printed in Hong Kong
20/PPHK/1

EXPLORER ACADEMY

MORE TO EXPLORE!

The world of the future comes alive in the thrilling seven-book series, full of danger, mystery, and amazing science. Join the adventure!

Check out more fun activity books featuring the characters and themes of Explorer Academy.

Watch videos, play a codebreaking game, and discover more at **exploreracademy.com**

AVAILABLE WHEREVER BOOKS ARE SOLD

© 2020 National Geographic Partners, LLC

UNDER THE *Stars*

NATIONAL GEOGRAPHIC